Unveiling Our Passions

Copyright

Paperback ISBN: 978-1-961966-20-8

Published by: Carxander Publishing
Minnesota

Disclaimer

The books in this series are based completely on dreams that I've had or that one of the other two people in my relationship has had. They all have a little bit of real life thrown in so that you, the reader, can get to know us a little bit better.

These books can and should be read as standalone books. There isn't an order to them. All of the characters in the books are the same, as they are all based on characters from real life.

As you read these books, please keep in mind that other than the characters and the city they are based in, these books are not connected to other books in the series. They aren't a continuation of other books. They are all novellas based on dreams that revolve around the same characters.

As you keep that in mind, please enjoy reading this book. I do hope you will also read the others in this series and love them as much as I loved writing them!

Opening Quote

Show no mercy. Show no love. No saving me. You're out for blood. 'Cause you're a cannibal, a cannibal. You're a cannibal, a cannibal. Fight like hell, you won't let go. You leave me naked in my bones. 'Cause you're a cannibal, a cannibal. You're a cannibal, a cannibal. You're the darkest part of me. You choke me out 'til I can't breathe. Oh, now there's nothing left of me. You're a cannibal. You're a cannibal

Cannibal by Citizen Soldier

Chapter One

☆ Mariah ☆

(Two Years Ago)

"Why can't you just help me?" he says to me as he stands over me. *I cower in my chair. "I don't know how to make appointments and fill prescriptions. That's what you're supposed to do."*

"I said I would," I whisper. *"I just... can't right now."* I can't because I've already been struggling today. I barely got out of bed. I can't even concentrate on writing, even though I have a deadline coming up.

"Right. Because you're so busy."

"No, Rodney. It's because I'm having a hard day," I say quietly. I don't look up at him. I try to stay focused on my laptop, but I really just want to curl into myself.

"I'm the one who goes out and works all day. How is your day so hard?"

I don't say anything because he's right. I can't go out and work. It's the same old argument over and over. I try to explain my depression, my anxiety, my panic. It does nothing. He doesn't understand. No one does. Everyone just thinks I'm lazy and crazy.

Fat.

I blink back tears and try to fight off the voice in my head. The one *that's always trying to bring me down. The one that constantly tells me I'm not good enough. The world would be better off without me in it. I should just quit. Everything. Being a writer. Going outside. I'm a burden.*

"I don't know what to do for you. I can't help you. I don't know how to." He leaves the room, and I sink further and further into myself.

All I need, all I've ever needed, is support. Understanding. Maybe a fucking hug while I cry. I take a breath and start working on digging myself out of the black abyss once more. The walls are only getting steeper, though. I know I'm not going to be able to do this forever.

I sniffle.

I don't want to be this way. I don't really even know where it stems from. Maybe being molested as a child. That's when the anxiety started. The depression. I became very quiet. But I blocked so much of what happened to me out of my head. I still dealt with the depression. I still dealt with the anxiety. But I fought the panic. I shoved it all away and hid it from everyone. I never showed a single sign of my struggle. It's just not the way my family works. Showing a weakness is an easy way to earn ridicule.

So, I never did. I still don't. Even the night I took a knife to my wrist. No one knew it. Not even my best friend. No one knew how close I was. No one knew I had that blade to my wrist. No one knew how far I'd fallen.

And no one knew the one thing that brought me back to reality was a picture of my grandmother. Her devastation if I'd done it.

I'm back to that place. I'm losing it. I can't fight it off like I used to. I'm nearing forty. I feel like a damn child.

I get up and head for the kitchen to make dinner. I'm wearing a pair of my favorite short shorts and my favorite t-shirt. It's hot in Duluth, Minnesota, at this time of year. Humid. My stomach is just barely sticking out of my t-shirt. Before I have a chance to pull it down, I already know he's going to make a comment.

"What's that?" Rodney asks as he pokes my stomach when I walk by him. I sniffle and say nothing. I try to tune him out, but he doesn't make it easy. He never does. "Just saying hi to it. God, you can't even take a joke."

I hug myself as I start dinner and do the dishes. I force his words out of my mind and try to focus on literally anything else. After dinner is started, I slip into the bathroom and close the door. Partially to calm myself. And partially because I need to actually use it.

But my solitude, no matter how brief it typically is, doesn't last longer than a few seconds. I hear him get out of his chair. I hear him walk to the kitchen. I hear him grumbling something about dinner burning right before he pushes open the door as I'm doing my business. I shoot him a glare.

"Closing the door? Hiding something? It smells like skunk weed in here. Are you smoking it?"

My mouth actually drops. "I've never smoked that shit, and you know it!" I shriek, finally fed up with everything he's said and done today. It's not the first time I've lost myself and screamed at him. "I can't even stand the smell of cigarette smoke! It makes me physically ill! How can you stand there and ask me if I'm smoking skunk weed when you know the smell of that makes me even more sick?"

"Wow! What's wrong with you? You must have your period or something."

I shove the door closed before he sees me burst into tears. "I hate him," I whisper to myself. "Fucking hate him."

"You gonna sit in there all day? You're burning stuff! Should I stir this? I don't know how to cook this!"

"You don't know how to cook spaghetti? It's just like macaroni! You make that!" I retort. I rub my head. The panic headache is setting in. The one I get after I've spent all day panicking and fighting with my demon. I can't handle the fight with him tonight, too.

I just want to scream at him. I want to throw a tantrum. I want to say the things he says to me back to him. But I know it wouldn't help because he doesn't understand. When I married him, I guess I wasn't aware of how much his medical issues affected his head. I thought he'd still know the difference between right and wrong. I thought he'd be able to learn from his mistakes, but I was wrong.

I was wrong because no matter how many times I've begged him not to call me a bitch, he does it. I've asked him not to touch my stomach or shake my flab and say the things he does because it makes me feel fatter than I already am. I know I'm not perfect. Weighing over three hundred pounds, isn't what I wanted for myself. But mental health plays a huge role in that.

One more thing no one understands.

"Can you spray? It stinks."

I shake my head and try to compose myself. "I just peed."

"It smells like a skunk."

I defiantly don't spray as I open the door and step out. He sprays and closes the door. I roll my eyes and say nothing to him. I finish dinner and let him dish his own food up as I walk back to my writing den. My place of solitude. I curl into my chair.

"You're not eating?"

"Nope."

"Whatever. Don't then."

Why would I eat after he just called me fat? Maybe he didn't say the words, but the meaning is there. It's always there. Like when he says we need to start going to the gym. Or when he stares at me when I'm trying to do things to better myself and says stuff to me about how I'm having a hard time getting off the floor. Or when I'm in front of him with no shirt and he tells me to put clothes on.

"This chair smells different. Who did you have over today?"

I shake my head and put in my earphones. "No one. I hate people and have no friends. Why the fuck would I have anyone over?" I turn up my music and drown him out. He loves accusing me of cheating on him.

The music drowns out his voice, but it doesn't work to drown out the demon in my head. The one who keeps telling me I'm not worth it. To just end it. I'm stupid for believing I deserve love from anyone. I close my eyes and give into the berating because my demon is right. He's always right.

I don't deserve kindness or understanding. I don't deserve love…

(Present Day)

My eyes snap open. I clutch my chest. My peace has been interrupted, but I'm not quite to the point of seeing who or what did it. I blink several times as I come back to myself. I stare, unseeing, at the sky and hug myself harder.

Tighter.

"You okay?" a deep voice asks me.

I blink a few more times and take several deep breaths before I turn and look into the most beautiful brown eyes I've ever seen. The man is sinfully gorgeous. Tattoos snake up his arms. He has washboard abs and muscles that I'm sure he works super hard to maintain. The blue swim trunks he's wearing are a little baggy, but even with him sitting down, I can see that his thighs are just as toned as the rest of him. His shorts are slung low on his hips. His short brown hair is messy. The scruff on his face is perfect. He looks like he just walked out of the male version of *Sports Illustrated's Swimsuit Edition.*

It takes a few moments for my head to catch up to my out of control heart. "U-um…" I rub my chest as I tear my eyes away from him. In the pool is another guy doing laps. I take another breath and look down at my hands. "I'm okay." It's then I realize that the delicious man next to me has a hand on my knee.

He squeezes it, effectively sending goosebumps all over my body. "You sure? You looked pretty lost there. And you're crying."

Mortified, I swipe at my eyes and shake my head. "Really. Just…" I sniffle and hold up my phone. "I was reading. There was a part that reminded me of something I went through. I got a little lost."

The mystery man studies me for a few moments before he lets my leg go. "I can understand that." He gives me a soft and sexy smile. "We all have our demons." He holds his hand out to shake mine. "I'm Matt."

I let out a breath before shakily putting my hand in his. I jump when he takes it. His hand is rough. Well worked. He definitely uses them a lot in whatever he does. But it's not the roughness that makes my eyes snap to his in surprise. It's the jolt I felt the very second his skin touched mine.

Jesus… Christ… Did he feel that?

His eyes give nothing away, but he doesn't drop my hand. Instead, he keeps watching me with those sultry, sexy eyes and panty melting smile.

I clear my throat and gently pull my hand away. I'm a little disappointed he let me. "Mariah," I say quietly.

"Mariah. A beautiful name for a beautiful girl." He smiles wider. Oh, he knows exactly what he does. He's dangerous, and he's well aware. He nods towards the pool, breaking eye contact with me for the first time. "That's DJ." He turns and leans back on the pool chair. He puts the sunglasses perched on top of his head over his eyes as he settles. "So, Mariah. How long have you lived here?"

"Oh, um…" I nibble the inside of my cheek. "A couple of years now." I focus back on the phone in my hand.

"Where are you from? Minnesota?"

I snap my head to him. My eyes widen. "How did you guess that?"

He chuckles. "Your accent. It's a little harder to place, considering you have a bit of a Southern twang, but Minnesotans have a very distinct accent. I grew up in North Dakota. Fairly close to the border with Minnesota, actually. I guess I just got used to hearing it when we went into Fargo for anything."

I blink at him, but he doesn't turn his head towards me, so I turn away again and lean my head back on my own pool chair. "You're really observant." I don't add that it's very unnerving.

"Part of my job."

I chuckle. "CIA operative?"

"Fuck no. Interpol," he responds without missing a beat.

I laugh, but sober pretty quickly. "Wait. Really?"

It's his turn to laugh. "No. I'm a Lieutenant with the Gainesville

Police Department. DJ is a Captain."

I smile and relax a little more than I already was. Matt is really easy to talk to and alarmingly soothing. I haven't talked to hardly anyone the entire time I've lived in Gainesville. It's not only a way to protect myself, it's also the best way I know to keep my anxiety at bay.

I don't know why I haven't run away yet. I force myself to come down to the private pool that only residents of my apartment complex can use. There's no one down here between the hours of nine and ten in the morning. Typically anyway. If someone does come, I tend to quickly pack up and flee to the safety of my apartment.

I don't do well with people. I never really have, but it's gotten a lot worse over the past few years. I've watched from the sidelines, unable to do anything about it, as the person I used to be slowly faded away. I know full well that I'm a shell of who I used to be.

And I know a big part of it is because of *him*. My ex-husband. The man who I honestly believed loved me for me. For all of me. The man who I truly thought would support me as I did him. The man I thought I could talk to about anything. I thought he'd help me through it, just like I helped him through all of his ailments, including his heart surgery.

But that's not what I got.

It's not who he was.

Is.

It's not who he is.

"Earth to Mariah," Matt says quietly, lightly touching my arm.

I jolt again. Partially because I'd allowed myself to get lost in my thoughts again, but also because his touch does something to me that no other person I've ever been in contact with has done. It calms me. Brings me back to reality when my demon is trying to pull me into my own special brand of hell.

"Sorry," I whisper. "I'm pretty out of it today, I guess."

He lets his hand fall from my skin, and I'm instantly cold. I miss it. How do I miss something, like a touch, from a man I only just met?

"You don't need to be. It's pretty obvious you're having a hard day. If you want to talk, though, I've been told I'm a pretty good listener." He smiles that disarmingly sexy smile again, but he's not looking at me. His head is still leaned back on the pool chair as he enjoys the sun beating down on his golden and sculpted body.

I chuckle again and shake my head. "I'm pretty sure you don't want to know. It's a long and very painful story."

"Sometimes, getting it out is the best medicine. It helps you because it's not bottled up. And it might help the person you're talking to as well. He'll know why you keep drifting off, and how to circumvent it."

I smile and glance at him. "Well, you're definitely persistent. I'll give you that."

He shrugs as the grin widens. "Perk of the job."

Before I can say anything more and continue to enjoy the easy banter I have going on with the sexiest man I've ever seen in my entire life, I catch a glimpse of a group of college guys heading our way. I glance at my phone with a quiet sigh. It's nearly eleven. I was out of it for a lot longer than I thought.

The college guys look pretty rambunctious. Obnoxious. They're pushing each other around and loudly laughing as they head directly for the pool. For some reason, I get very nervous. Usually, I'd say it has a lot to do with the fact that there is a large group of people coming my way, but that's not it this time.

No.

It's the way they're acting. The way a few of them have me in their eyesight. The way they're catcalling and whistling at me. The way the guy in front of them all is looking me up and down with a look in his eye that is far from hunger or longing or craving or attraction.

It's danger.

Something so scary that I physically shiver, even though it has to be close to ninety degrees out here.

They all drop their towels on a couple of the pool chairs. Most of them jump into the water, but some of them don't. And the ones who don't have their eyes trained directly on me. My heart starts beating so quickly that I can hear it in my head. It's roaring. My vision starts to blur.

"Um... I... need to go," I squeak out in a whisper to Matt. I clutch my phone to my chest.

"They're not going to hurt you," he says quietly back to me as the man Matt called DJ gets out of the pool.

I pause as I stand. Much like Matt, DJ is a tall drink of water. He's just as muscular. He's got the same short hair. A perfect amount of scruff. His body is so well toned that it takes my breath away. He doesn't have tattoos, but he doesn't need them. I've always thought tattoos made a man look a little dangerous and a lot sexy. But looking at DJ, I'm fairly certain if he had tattoos, the entire world would spontaneously combust.

Then again, Matt has them and the world is still turning.

I shake my head. I can't think clearly. DJ's gorgeous jade eyes are on me. Matt's sexy brown ones are burning a hole through me. Three of the college guys who entered the pool area are standing in a semicircle and staring at me.

My head is spinning.

I feel like I might pass out because of how dizzy I am.

"I need to leave," I whisper.

Not looking back, I flee.

I run all the way to my apartment building and don't stop until I reach the elevator. Punching the button to the top floor, I pray I get to my sanctuary before the panic takes over. I feel it. I know it's coming. I won't be able to stop it. I never can.

But at least no one will look at me like I'm insane.

Crazy.

A freak.

At least I can fall apart without the fear of people laughing at me.

Without anyone standing over me screaming that they don't know what to do…

I burst through my door in a rush, barely hearing it slam closed behind me. My breathing picks up as I stand frozen in my living room. I grip my phone tighter in my hand as the room spins. Or maybe it's me.

As I try to take deep breaths, I feel the walls closing in…

The darkness is creeping over me again.

Slowly.

And this time, with my heart pounding in my ears, I know I can't stop it…

Chapter Two

☆ DJ ☆

"Well, at least that wasn't weird," I say as I dry off. "Who was that?"

"Uh. Our future spouse? Fuck me. She's gorgeous." Matt clears his throat as he glances at me. "Mariah is her name."

I glance over my shoulder at the idiot college guys behind me. Four of them are doing flips into the pool. I roll my eyes. Matt and I have been perfectly content living in an apartment since we're never home. It's the downfall to being a cop. We can't even keep plants alive.

Recently, we've decided a house is better for us, though. This place used to be pretty quiet until new management came on. Now, we can't get the fucking noise shut down any more than we can get someone from maintenance to fix anything. We do it ourselves, but if we're going to do that, we may as well just get our own fucking house.

I turn back to Matt and chuckle because his eyes haven't left Mariah as she quickly makes her way to the doors to the building. "Looks like we aren't the only ones who are captivated by her."

Matt looks at me as Mariah disappears into the building. "Yeah. I saw that." He glances over his shoulder at the guys. The three who were watching Mariah jump in the pool with their friends. "She was pretty freaked out by them."

"Makes me wonder why." I finish drying off, my heart pounding, and follow Matt in the direction Mariah went. "Took quite a bit for me to stop myself from chasing her. Can't put my finger on why."

"You and me both."

"So, future spouse? She must have laid a spell on you," I tease. "Last I checked, we're a couple or something."

Matt barks out a laugh. "She's prettier than you."

I grin. "I can't even deny you that."

Matt and I are bisexual. We've been in a relationship with each other for years. We've shared women during that time. We've never been with anyone else without each other since we've been together. We're committed to each other, but we've always wanted a woman to complete us and our relationship dynamic. We haven't found her.

Until today. I'm with Matt on this girl. Mariah sent those proverbial butterflies into flight. I only barely glimpsed her, but the girl is gorgeous. Even with the fear filling her pretty blue eyes, and the fight or flight instincts taking control over her. My chest painfully constricts.

"My money is on anxiety. I bet having everyone around her like that scared her," Matt says, slicing through my thoughts.

"All I know is I want to get to know her better. Just… something about her."

Matt rubs his chest. "With you on that."

I raise an eyebrow. "You okay?"

"She took off so fast. Just feel like something is wrong."

Matt opens the door for me and follows me in as I nod. I always get a kick out of it. We're both chivalrous men. I'm just over fifty and from Texas. I've always said it's the Southern gentleman in me. But I met my match with Matt. He's just over forty and from North Dakota, but he's lived in Gainesville for many, many years. Maybe nearly as long as me. I'm going on twenty-five years in this city.

Matt always says men in the North are far more gentlemanly than us Southern boys. It's a running joke between the two of us. I'll never allow him to truly believe that shit. Southern men have a reputation to protect.

We jog up the stairs to our fourth floor apartment. As we're walking down the hall, we hear gasping coming from the apartment across from ours. I glance at Matt with a raised eyebrow. He mimics my expression and nods to the door the whimpers, sobs, and squeaky crying is coming from.

"Who lives there?" Matt asks.

"I honestly have no idea. That older lady moved out a couple of years ago. We were at SWAT training when the new person moved in. I haven't seen whoever it is."

Matt looks at me. "The name on the mailbox for this apartment is M. Carter. Mariah?"

I shrug, but I'm suddenly surpassing mild worry and filled with a sense of dread. "There are a lot of names that begin with the letter M."

"Yeah, I guess. But she was experiencing anxiety down there. I think this is her." Matt knocks lightly on the door. I'm glad he did it because I was about to. "Mariah?" he calls softly. "It's Matt. You okay?"

There's a hiccup quickly followed by a gasp. I look at Matt when things fall silent. "The fuck?"

Matt presses his ear against the door. After a few moments he sighs. "I think she went to her room."

"Every instinct in me is screaming to not let her be alone." The feeling alarms me.

"Well, I can't force her to open the door. Let's get changed. We'll try again after."

I run a hand through my still wet hair. "Explain to me why I feel like I'm being ripped apart. I didn't even talk to her, yet my stomach is fucking tight. My heart feels like it's being ripped out of my chest. Instant connection to her. What the fuck is this shit?"

"Something neither of us have felt about anyone except for each other. That's what it is." Matt lets us into our apartment and closes the door behind us.

I turn and look at him. We're close to the same height. He's six feet four. I'm six feet three. I don't have to look up at all to look in his eyes. "I don't like this. Something is going on."

"Cop instincts, DJ. Go take a shower. I'll get you some clothes. Maybe make something for lunch and bring it over there."

I head to the shower, intent on making it quick. I feel like we need to be with Mariah right now. She may not know she needs us. Maybe she doesn't need us. But she sure as fuck needs someone. Holy hell, I want that to be us.

"That's a good idea. There's some chicken noodle in the freezer. Warm that up," I call over my shoulder as I disappear in the bathroom.

Not more than five minutes later, I'm stepping out and drying off. I grab the gray sweats and black t-shirt Matt laid out for me and slip them on, foregoing underwear completely. I run my fingers through my hair and head out to the kitchen.

Matt has changed into gray sweatpants and his favorite red Captain America t-shirt. He's making sandwiches as the soup warms. I raise an eyebrow when he starts cutting them into small squares.

"The fuck are you doing?"

Matt laughs. "Finger sandwiches. You never had these as a kid?"

"I grew up with a dick father who drank more than either of us ate. Remember? Most of my food consisted of tuna from a can, pork and beans, and ramen noodles. I made mayo and mustard sandwiches."

Matt makes a face. "I still can't believe you turned out relatively normal."

I laugh. He's not wrong. My life wasn't easy. My dad was an abusive motherfucker who loved smacking me and my mother around. My mother died in a car wreck when I was ten, leaving me with his drunken ass. When he wasn't stumbling around, he was pissed off and taking it out on me. When he wasn't pissed off, he was passed out.

I got out as soon as I turned eighteen. I joined the Army. My father died while I was overseas. To this day, I don't feel bad for leaving. I sure as fuck don't feel anything for him. I'm happy he's gone. I hope he skipped Hell and went straight to the deepest depths of the hole he crawled out of. The same place the likes of Hitler and Bin Laden reside. I'm sure they're all having lots of fun together.

Matt grew up quite a bit differently than I did. His parents are pretty damn loving. His dad is a retired Marine. Tough, but he's still a good guy. Matt followed in his dad's footsteps and joined the Marines. We're both retired now and happily serving the people of Gainesville, Florida. He's a Lieutenant. I'm a Captain. Neither of us get to patrol much anymore, but when we do, it's enjoyable for us.

The two of us have been together for almost twenty years now. I was Matt's training officer. We became fast friends. It didn't take long for it to become more than friendship. We knew pretty quickly we were meant to be together. We kept our relationship under wraps for many, many, many years. To this day, not many people in the department know Matt and I are a couple. And if they do, they keep their mouths fucking shut like they should.

Truthfully, our life together has been peaceful and blissful. We share women when we want one. We have each other when we don't. We'd be happy on our own and content in the life we lead, but we do want that special woman to complete us. Does it seem strange to most? Fuck. Probably. But neither of us really give a shit. We're going to live our life how we want to regardless of the opinions of others.

Just like we have the past twenty years.

I sigh and start stirring the soup as I glance at the door. "Maybe I should knock until she opens up."

"DJ, don't. That's bound to scare the shit out of her. She seemed okay. As soon as she heard the knock, the gasping stopped. Which means that panic attack was subsiding. We need to give her a little time."

I just nod, but I don't like the feelings I have going on right now. I don't like that I feel she needs us. I don't like that I have strong feelings for a woman I've never met. I've never believed in love at first sight. Hell, I don't even think I fell for Matt when I first saw him. Though, he'd probably say something different.

I close my eyes and lean against the counter. I need to get a grip. I'm not thinking clearly at all. I did have strong feelings right out of the gate for Matt. I fell hard and fast. So did he. Was it love at first sight? Who the fuck knows? But the feelings were there. Just like they are now. I knew early on he was mine to love and protect. Cherish.

Same feelings I'm having right now for her.

Fuck.

"Give me something to do, Matt. I'm losing my fucking mind over a girl I've never met." I open my eyes and move next to him.

"Okay." He smiles and kisses me before pointing to the counter. "Ham and cheese. Finish cutting them. The soup is almost finished. Wrap those in plastic wrap. Grab some drinks." He turns to the stove. I do what he says. "And if you think you're the only one losing your mind, you aren't, baby. I felt an instant connection to that girl. I know there's something happening, and I want to help her fight it, but we need to be tactful on this. I don't think she needs us coming on that strong."

I chuckle. "Really? Because I know you. You're not going to leave once we get over there. You're going to insist on taking care of her. That isn't strong?" I shoot him a grin over my shoulder as I wrap the sandwiches after I finish cutting them.

He laughs. "I said that strong. I didn't say strong. I think she needs someone to take control and show her that whatever the hell is going on, she has support and help. Guidance to help her through. A little dominance in her submissively led life."

I nearly choke as I whirl around to him. "Submissive?"

He nods as he stirs the soup and says nothing more. Matt and I are both dominant men. But we don't want a woman who is so submissive that she can't stand on her own two feet. So far, the women we've been with have been on two very opposite ends of the spectrum. Either so submissive that she can't speak for herself, or so independent and fierce that, while we admired her for all she's accomplished in life and are proud of her for knowing everything she wants and not being afraid to take it, she just wasn't for us.

When Matt uses the word submissive, he means she's the perfect balance we've been looking for. It makes me wish I said fuck the laps earlier and followed Matt's lead. I should have sat down and talked to the woman that captivated us both. Unfortunately for me, I needed the laps to work off some of my frustration over a case Matt and I caught yesterday. I thought I had time to talk to her, too.

I can't help but chuckle as Matt transfers the soup into a container easier for us to carry. "You realize how fucked up this is? We've been waiting our whole lives for a woman like her. And she has no idea. We're going to come off as obsessed assholes."

"We're going to come off as two guys who care about a woman and want to help her through whatever she's going through. She's not going to have a clue that we want her as much as we do because that isn't what she needs. That will come later." Matt turns and puts his hands on my shoulders. "You're feeling this way because you're a protective and possessive motherfucker. But we need to be tactful about this, DJ." He lets me go.

I shake my head as if I'm coming out of a trance or something. "I know you're right."

Matt grabs a couple of hot pads and takes the container with the soup. He nods towards the platter with the sandwiches. I take it and tuck the drinks between my arm and body. I open the door for Matt and make sure I have keys. I take a deep breath after closing the door and assuring myself it's locked.

"Knock. I'll talk," Matt says.

I nod and knock on Mariah's door. She doesn't answer. I suppose I didn't figure she would. I press my ear against the door, but I'm met with silence. "She couldn't have snuck out on us."

Matt shakes his head. "No. I would've heard her." He nods to the door. I knock again, a little harder. "Mariah? It's Matt and DJ. We're not going away until we know you're okay."

It takes her a few more knocks, but she finally opens the door. Her eyes are puffy from crying. Her cheeks are red. Her pretty long hair falls in tangles down her back. Her eyes don't meet ours. She keeps them on the ground and has a grip on the door that makes me believe she'll fall over if she even thinks of letting it go.

My heart shatters for her. All I can think of is figuring out what the hell this girl went through to put her in this state. I want to sweep her in my arms and kiss it all away. The pain. The hurt. I want to show her that whatever happened in her past doesn't define who she is today.

"I'm… fine…," she says. Her voice cracks. It's barely above a whisper.

"You're far from okay, honey," I say quietly, as soothingly as possible.

"We brought soup," Matt says in the same tone as me. "You don't need to tell us what happened out there." Matt dips his head when Mariah looks up at him. She's still teary, but hopeful. "Yet," he finishes.

I give her one of my prized smiles. "How about you let us in? You can get settled on that very comfy looking couch right there." I nod to a large, plush, off-white, L-shaped couch fitted snugly against the wall in her living room. I smile a little wider when her gorgeous deep blue eyes meet mine. "We'll get this soup and these sandwiches set up. And then we can watch a movie."

She bites her lip. "Oh. Um… I…" She glances over her shoulder and clears her throat. She takes a breath and looks back at us. "Tampa is playing the Vikings… I… was… just going to watch it." She looks down at the ground again. "Try to get my head on right."

I just stare at her for a moment. My dick twitches. I clear my throat and shake my head. "You're a football fan?"

She looks up at us shyly. "Mmhmm. It helps my…" She shakes her head and takes a deep breath. "We can watch a movie. It's okay." She stands aside and opens the door wider for us to enter. This girl can't possibly be any more perfect. Beautiful and a football fan. I might already be in love.

"Are you kidding?" Matt leads me inside and heads straight for the kitchen. "Tampa's my favorite team." He looks at her and narrows his eyes with a teasing smile. "Wait. Don't you dare tell me you live in Florida and plan to root for the fucking Vikings. I'll take my soup away. I have to deal with this one enough when the damn Dolphins play." He flicks a finger at me after he sets the soup down.

Mariah's eyes light up, and she giggles. Actually fucking giggles. The sound is melodic and lifts my heart. I never knew I needed her giggle in my life until now. Fuck me. I'm making a vow here and now to make her giggle for the rest of my life.

She runs her thumb under her eye. "Well, the truth? I hate the Vikings. I'm still pissed off at them for the kick heard 'round the world in the NFC Championship game of ninety-eight. But I might just root for them to take you up on that challenge." She smiles softly and looks up at Matt.

I fight the twitch of my dick once more. "You might be the death of me, little one." I reach down and use the counter to hide myself from her as I adjust myself. She gives me a confused look, but Matt sees exactly what I'm doing. And judging by the tent in his sweats, her teasing has the same effect on him.

Matt grins. "I like this joking Mariah."

Mariah blushes and ducks her head. "I was just going to grab some taco dip I made out of the fridge. And some Fritos." She tucks a strand of hair behind her ear as she starts for the fridge. I really wish I could have done that.

"Is it in the fridge?" I ask, quickly turning. I don't want her to see my growing issue or Matt's. "Go sit down. Turn on the game. We'll be in there in a second."

"O-oh… Okay."

I look over my shoulder and let out a groan only Matt can hear as I open the fridge. I take out the taco dip. After a few moments of willing my hard on to behave, I bring the dip, the chips she wanted, and the sandwiches we brought to the coffee table in front of her couch as she settles, watching us both. Matt finds bowls and pours the soup. I find spoons and help him bring the bowls and the drinks into the living room just as the game is starting.

We hand Mariah a bowl as we sit down on either side of her. She's quiet as she watches the game, but I can see her sneaking glances at us both like she doesn't know what to make of us. I'm okay with that, though.

As long as she starts to understand that we're not going anywhere.

Chapter Three

☆ Matt ☆

(Two Weeks Later)

I slam the door to our apartment as hard as I can as I glare at the motherfucker leaving Mariah's apartment. He smirks at me, and it takes all of my willpower not to *shoot* him. For the past couple of weeks, DJ and I have gotten considerably closer to Mariah, but we've apparently been friend-zoned because Mr. College Asshole From the Pool Who Was Staring At Our Girl And Making Her Nervous As Fuck has been spending an awful lot of time with her.

I look at my watch. Six in the morning. I give Mariah's door a vicious glare capable of melting steel. There's only one reason a man would be leaving a woman's house this early with his shoes in his hand and the belt on his jeans unbuckled.

"I'm gonna puke," I murmur as the bile rises up my throat. I quickly bend over with my hands on my knees and close my eyes.

DJ rubs my back. "Yeah. Me too. What the hell is that asshole doing with her?"

It takes several deep breaths for me to compose myself enough to not make a mess of this hallway. It takes even longer for me to not storm into Mariah's apartment demanding answers while I tell her she belongs to us.

The question DJ asked is one we've both been asking since the day after the football game we watched with Mariah. By the time the night was over, Mariah had turned into this fun-loving woman. She was laughing. Blushing. She even opened up to us about her anxiety and panic. She told us what happened at the pool that day. Thanked us for helping her come down. Since that night, we've spent a lot of time with her. We've gotten to know more about her. Our feelings have grown stronger.

There are times we both think Mariah is starting to feel the same for us. She flirts. She snuggles close. We catch her watching us when she thinks we aren't paying attention. And she quickly looks away when she thinks she's been caught. She's opened up more and more each day. DJ and I not only know about the pool and why she ran, but we also know about her being sexually assaulted as a kid.

I bet that fucking asshole doesn't know that.

It pisses us off even more knowing that Mariah has been spending a lot of time with the college douchenozzle. He's ordered takeout for them. One time it was a pizza. I saw it when I came home. Pizza makes her sick. It sets off her acid reflux and sends her straight to the bathroom. There's only one kind of pizza in this city that she can tolerate. Pizza Hut ain't it.

I run my fingers through my hair as I stand up. "I'll admit I fucked up. We shouldn't have taken it slow. We should've claimed her the second we fucking saw her."

"Matt. Come on. You know better than that. You were right. That would've scared the shit out of her. She said it herself. He didn't swoop in trying to play the hero. He talked to her down at the pool without his friends. He soothed her when they showed up and made her nervous. And judging by what we were just unfortunate witnesses to, it looks like things are a bit more serious. You and I need to regroup. Because no way in all of fucking Hell will I allow our girl to be with that motherfucker. She belongs with us."

I let out a low growl as I follow DJ down the hall. Neither of us like elevators, but we haven't been sleeping well either. Ever since Mariah told us that she was going to have him over for a movie. I don't even know the guy's name. All I know is he's all over what's ours. And he does it intentionally. Every time we're around, he stands closer to her. Touches her. Leans in and whispers something in her ear that makes her giggle.

That's *our* fucking giggle. *Ours* to listen to. Her hair is *ours* to touch. Her eyes are *ours* to stare into and drown in. And what's more? She's fucking *ours* to hold. *Ours* to snuggle with. Her flirting and shyness belongs to *us*.

I growl again as we step into the elevator. "If I punched the wall, you think they'd kick us out?"

DJ chuckles. "They'd sure as fuck make you pay for the damage. And then I'd have to write up a report because my subordinate lost his temper and punched an elevator wall, damaging private property. So really, you'd be making more work for your boyfriend. Who you're supposed to love more than anything."

I grin and shake my head. "I'll never understand how you do that."

DJ leans in and kisses me deeply. His tongue twines with mine, and my hands automatically find his ass. I moan into the kiss as I squeeze him. My body relaxes into him. All except my dick. DJ has a way of making me hard just by looking at me. His kisses turn my cock into steel.

DJ grips my hip. His lips upturn into a small smile as he slowly pulls away. "Getting you out of your head is like my super power."

I laugh as he steps away just as the doors open. We both walk off the elevator and head for the front door, but we don't make it far. One of our friends is standing near the mailboxes hugging herself as she furiously chews her lip.

I raise an eyebrow as we stop next to her. "Lyric. What are you doing up so early, sweetheart?" I ask her.

She jumps as she looks up at me and DJ. "U-um…" She glances towards the door before shaking her head and turning to hug us both.

Lyric Sharpe is a petite woman. She has curves in all the right places and is truly gorgeous. When we speak of natural submissives, she's who we speak of. She needs guidance in both life and the bedroom. She thrives on the dominance. But she's nowhere near a little frail girl. She runs her own company. She's a graphic designer and creates logos and branding for giant corporations all the way down to the smallest of self-published authors. She's figured out a sliding price scale. She doesn't post prices anywhere. She bases her prices on the project and what her clients can afford.

Lyric is one of the most intelligent women I've ever had the pleasure of meeting. She's one of mine and DJ's closest friends. Hell, we might have ended up with her if she didn't already have a boyfriend. He's a bartender at a prestigious club here in Gainesville. Lyric constantly teases us that he works less and makes more than us.

We got to talking about it, though, and she's fucking right. Even with our overtime, her boyfriend makes a lot more than us with his tips and hourly wage. Now the joke is that DJ and I are in the wrong profession. We should be working as bartenders. Or Graphic Designers because Lyric makes more than we do, too.

DJ and I both hug Lyric tight. "What happened, honey?" DJ asks. "You're staring at the door like you just watched a ghost walk out of it."

She sighs and pulls back. "I couldn't sleep. Kieran had a late night. He got home like an hour ago. I didn't sleep at all. I'm exhausted. I thought I'd go for a walk or something. I was grabbing the mail on the way back upstairs. I heard a couple of jerks talking about some bullshit bet they have going on with this girl. Something about how long it will take for one of them to fuck her. So fucking sickening."

DJ and I share a look. I cross my arms over my chest, not liking where this is going. "Do you know who it was, honey? Or who they were talking about?"

Lyric looks up at me with some of that British fire in her eyes. She's from the United Kingdom. Her accent is as adorable as she is, but she's a fucking spitfire when she wants to be. And it looks like now is the time. Her lines have been crossed. It takes a lot to piss her off, but when she reaches that point, God help the fucking world.

"Yeah. You know that girl you two have been talking about?" Lyric glares at the door. "Her. The two guys who were talking about it are the two assholes around her most. The main guy is the one that you two want to use for target practice."

DJ sighs as I seethe. "Are you going to be around today?" DJ asks.

"Of course," Lyric says, looking up at him. "You know I hate people." She gestures to the door. "Point made about the reason why. Stupid ass sucking cockmuppet dirt lickers."

I can't help but laugh. Lyric makes up some incredibly insulting names for people she doesn't like, and I'm all here for it. I've stolen a few from her. Cockmuppet is one of my personal favorites, but I might steal ass sucking dirt licker.

DJ grins and chuckles. "Mariah usually heads to the pool in the morning. Can you and Kieran be down there? Keep an eye on her? Don't let her go anywhere with the fuck stick. Tell her you have a new design to show her."

"Done and done," Lyric agrees. "I actually have one I've only just finished. My first ever fantasy cover. I'll show her that one." She pauses as she yawns and rubs her eyes. "I'm going to try and get a couple hours of sleep, but we'll be down there. Kieran will understand."

"Thank you, sweet girl." I pull her into a hug. DJ wraps his arms around us both. We let her go after a few moments, and she heads for the elevator with her mail.

I've never been so grateful to have Lyric in our corner as I am today. She's one of our best friends. We're incredibly close to her and Kieran, her boyfriend. But knowing that she'll watch out for Mariah for us until we're back and can talk to her makes things a little easier on me.

Because I'm pissed. And judging from DJ's clenched fists, I'd say he's feeling the same.

"Squad Four," a female voice says over our handheld radios attached to our belts.

"I'm on my way in," DJ answers.

"10-4," dispatch acknowledges.

The interruption sends my mind back to the entire reason DJ and I are heading into work this early. Our night crew caught our main suspect in a murder we've been unable to solve. The case pissed me off in general. But it was not having a suspect that upset me the most. I hate not being able to give a family closure quickly.

The case involves an eighteen-year-old college student. A freshman at the University of Florida. She tried out for the cheerleading squad when an unexpected opening occurred. One of the main girls hurt her ankle. The new captains made the mistake of not having a backup list with girls on it who could be called in in events like this. They were forced to hold tryouts.

By all appearances, the case looks as if one of the girls trying out got jealous that our victim made the cut. Our victim was found in her dorm room. There was definitely a struggle. We found scratches over her and a fake acrylic nail sticking out of her skin. There was even a message written on the mirror in pink lipstick that said something about getting what she deserved because she should have known she'd never make it as a cheerleader.

Unfortunately for the murderer, the scene was so obviously staged, it was comical to those of us with a trained eye. The nail was taken out of a box of fake nails our victim had in her makeup case. The perpetrator stuck it into her skin to make it look like it came from a female. The lipstick was the victim's lipstick. The lab matched it to what she was wearing at the time and everything. There were signs of sexual assault that were proven upon further investigation.

DJ and I climb into my truck. We don't often drive to work together because there's never a guarantee that we'll be going home at the same time, but that won't be the case today. We'd already decided we're calling it an early day. Now, we have even more reason to.

"I knew there was something about this entire situation with that motherfucker," I rumble as I start driving towards our Headquarters building.

"Asshole is about to learn a lesson. I'll tell you that right now. I'm going to rip his dick off, shove it down his throat, and use him for target practice while he chokes on his balls."

I chuckle but say nothing. The mention of his dick has put unpleasant images in my head. Things like her underneath him while he plunges himself into her. Her riding him on that comfy white couch I've already claimed a spot on. Him making her come.

It's all thoughts I'm sure are running through DJ's head. He's fallen just as silent as me. Only his eyes are squeezed shut, and he's pinching the bridge of his nose. I'd probably be doing the same damn thing if I wasn't navigating Gainesville's streets.

I sigh. Damn this case. With the information Lyric gave us about this all being a sick fucking game, DJ and I would have called sick. We would've marched to her apartment and banged on the door until she opened.

Then we would've kissed her senseless, claiming her as our own like we should have done two fucking weeks ago.

My head keeps telling me that it's too late, but my heart isn't in agreement. My heart says it's never too late to right a wrong. I was wrong in believing taking things slow is how we needed to approach this. We should have made our interest in her clear from the beginning. Flirting isn't enough. Everyone flirts. Even if they don't mean to and don't realize it's happening.

It's obvious that it's part of Mariah's new routine with us. Flirt. Banter. Cuddle. Talk. We've never made it clear to her that we're interested in her as anything more than friends, so I can't be pissed off feeling like we've been friend-zoned. That's how we've made her feel.

"It's time we started over with her, DJ." I shake my head. "Time to be honest. Tell her our intentions."

"Matt, stop. Stop beating yourself up over this. We both made the decision to keep things slow and not push her. Were we wrong? No. I honestly don't think so. Because we're going to be the ones there for her to cushion the blow she's about to go through. It's through us that she met Lyric, Luca and Kieran. She has a circle. She may not know she needs one, but she'll be happy she does soon. We have the information we wanted. We know why he's been after her. It fucking sucks, but we know. We can deal with it. We just need to get through this shit first."

I pull into the parking garage and change the subject because if I don't, I'll turn around and say fuck this day. "I still don't think this guy is our guy," I say. "Just doesn't fit the bill. I know he's our main suspect, but it just doesn't make sense to me."

"I agree. But you know how this works. Haul him in. Ask our questions. Gain more info and clues. Hopefully, by the end of this, we'll have more to go on."

"I still think it was the boyfriend," I grumble.

DJ chuckles. "Well, according to literally everyone we talked to, she didn't have one."

"Well, people lie."

DJ shrugs as we get out of the truck. "I agree with that, too. But we need to look at this as a whole. She was quiet. She had no roommates. She had one friend. And we're about to talk to him. So let's work this like the good fucking cops we are and trust that our friend has our girl until we can get home."

I follow him through the garage and to our office in the building with a nod. He's right. I want to give this family closure and solve this case. Hopefully, we can get the information we need.

And then I'm going to fucking destroy the college asshole fucking with our girl.

Chapter Four

☆ Mariah ☆

"I like this bikini on you," Camden rumbles in my ear appraisingly as he hugs me and sways back and forth with me.

I blush. "Thank you," I whisper into his hard and smooth chest.

I'll admit I'm completely smitten with Camden. Who wouldn't be? Camden is gorgeous. He's tall, well-built, and he doesn't look bad without a shirt. He smells so good. Almost like the woods after a fresh rain. He's musky. He's a lot younger than me. He's a senior at the University of Florida. So are his friends. I don't really like them, but I like him.

And he's into me.

I'm glad I gave him a chance. Two weeks ago, after I ran from the pool before anyone could see me break, I went through one of the worst panic attacks I've had in a long time. My demon was talking shit so much. He was saying things I've been so good at ignoring.

But I fought. I fought so hard to not succumb this time. I did it. I came out of the darkness with less scars than usual. And the night with the football game, snacks, and the guys across the hall from me helped so much.

Matt and DJ.

They're both cops. They're both incredible men. They're so soothing. So kind and sweet. They're beyond dominant. It's a quality I had no idea I needed in my life until I met them. I've loved spending time with them and getting to know them these past couple of weeks. I know they're together, though, and that I can never have them.

They're bisexual, but it's obvious I'm not the type of woman they want because they've relegated me to the dreaded friend-zone. I've come to accept that. At least I get them as a friend, despite the instantaneous connection I felt with both of them. I'm sure those butterflies I get whenever I see them will never go away, but I'll take the banter and flirting if that's what they'll give me. I can't say I'm not sad about not being what they're looking for, though. I hate feeling things for people that they don't feel back.

Camden squeezes me tighter, running his hands up and down my bare back. The bikini he's so obsessed with is a gift from him. I've never worn one in my life. I've always been ashamed of my body. Even after losing as much weight as I have, I still feel like I'm not where I should be. I'm not as small as I should be. I know I have stretch marks. I'm not perfect. Not like the college girls Camden is used to.

Camden is only twenty-three. He's seventeen years younger than me. Ironically, he doesn't act it. He's easy to talk to. He's flirty. He's content to cuddle with me and watch movies. He understands that I can't do crowded places, and it's hard for me to go to the clubs and restaurants he's used to frequenting.

Much like DJ and Matt.

My grip tightens a little bit on Camden as he holds me like I'm the only thing in the world that matters to him. It's the biggest difference between him and Matt and DJ. I want both Matt and DJ. I feel awful about it. Dirty for wanting two men. Especially two men as intoxicating as them. But they don't want me like that.

Camden does.

He has made it clear since the day after the anxiety attack. I braved coming back down to the pool. Well, more like forced myself to do it. It was scary, but I didn't want to ruin my progress. The pool is the one place I go that's outside the sanctuary of my apartment. I decided that if they came again, I'd simply get up and leave.

But something made me stay.

Camden pulls back slowly but doesn't release me. He hooks his thumbs in the waistline of my bottoms. His fingertips grip my butt. I shiver. I'm still getting used to the fact that he sat down next to me, and I didn't run away. I talked to him. We had a good conversation. And since that day, we've seen each other every day. I'm enjoying spending time with him. I'm enjoying the attention he insists on lavishing on me. But mostly, I'm enjoying the fact that someone like him is genuinely interested in me. That our age difference doesn't matter at all to him.

He smiles down at me when I shyly look into his pretty, but dull blue eyes. They're not as piercing as DJ's jade ones. Not as vivid as Matt's coffee colored ones. I inwardly sigh and shake my head, keeping the smile on my face. They aren't interested in me. It's not fair to Camden for me to be thinking of them. He deserves more than that from me.

Am I just settling? Like I did for my ex?

Probably. Maybe. I don't even really know. I am attracted to Camden. I'd be crazy not to be. I was never that way with Rodney. I never felt this strong magnetic pull to him like I do with Camden. Or even Matt and DJ.

Maybe I'm just too relationship naive to know what I want or what I'm doing right now. I've only been in one real relationship. The others can't be considered relationships. One of them was in high school. It lasted a long time, but we only ever saw each other at school. Another was more of a friendship with a boyfriend/girlfriend title attached.

Rodney was the first person I actually slept with. We were married a year after we met. I know now I was pushed into it. My family basically told me that I needed to settle down and do what women are supposed to do. Get married and take care of my husband. I did it because I didn't know any better.

Camden runs his fingers through my hair. "Where do you keep going on me?"

I blink and shake my head. "I'm sorry," I say quietly as I look down at his chest. "I keep… drifting."

"I can tell. What I want to know is why."

I smile softly again as I look up at him. "I guess I'm thinking how strange it must be to you and all of your friends that you're with me." I bite my lip and take a breath, willing the demon away. I don't need to hear him telling me I'm not good enough for a man as attractive as Camden.

Camden cups my cheek. I lean into it as he makes me look at him. "I assure you, sweetie. No one thinks anything bad. I certainly don't. I don't give a shit about your age compared to mine. I really like you, Mariah."

"I know it's a conversation we've had before -"

"And it will probably be one we have again, but I don't care. I don't mind having it."

I hear a scoff behind me. Camden lets out a low growl as he looks over my head and shakes his. His fingertips tighten on my ass. I slowly turn around, but I really don't need to. I'd know that scoff anywhere.

Lyric Sharpe.

She's made it quite clear she doesn't like Camden in the slightest. So has her boyfriend Kieran. And there's no love lost between Camden and my two new friends. He doesn't like either of them either.

Lyric sits down with sunglasses perched on her adorable nose. Kieran pulls his pool chair close to hers and takes his own seat with a roll of his eyes as he puts his own sunglasses on. He says something I can't quite catch under his breath.

Camden tugs me closer. "Care to say that again? A little louder this time so I can actually hear you? Or maybe you just want to shut the fuck up."

"Camden," I whisper, silently pleading with him not to start a fight with Kieran. The last spat they had ended up with Kieran throwing a punch at him. The only reason Camden didn't retaliate is because I got in the middle and pushed him back.

Lyric tilts her head. "He said you're a lying fucking douchedick who should go run your games on someone else." She gives him a vicious glare over the rim of her sunglasses. "You know. Like one of the college whores who hang all over you."

Camden tenses. I hug him tighter as I look up at him. "Please don't," I plead.

He looks down at me with narrowed eyes. "Tell your girl to stop being a bitch, baby," he whispers in my ear only loud enough for me to hear. He taps my ass as he lets me go and dives into the pool with his friends.

"I also said she's not in the same fucking league as you and to find someone who is!" Kieran shouts when Camden resurfaces. This time, it's one of his friends who holds him back.

I sigh as I sit down. "I truly appreciate the two of you. I'm glad to have you both as friends since I don't have any. But you need to back off Camden." I take out my laptop and turn it on as I settle into the pool chair.

"Nope. I will not. That guy is a complete asshole. He's not for you," Lyric says with so much sass and confidence that I truly admire her.

I just nod with a soft smile as I focus on my laptop. I open my latest book I'm writing and focus completely on the words. Or at least try. Because if I don't, I'm going to think of Kieran's and Lyric's words. I'm going to analyze them. I'll know what they mean, but my demon will nitpick, and I'll start feeling that I'm wrong. That they mean something else.

That I'm not good enough for him.

Pretty enough.

Smart enough.

I shake my head and take a breath. I know that's not true. It isn't what they meant. Lyric and Kieran are amazing. They've become two of my favorite people. I'm already incredibly close to them both. Lyric has been a big help in me coming out of my shell. I met her one night when DJ and Matt told me it was their game and pizza night. They invited me to go with them.

Then ordered from the only pizza place I can eat at in this entire city. It's more expensive than the others, but they didn't bat an eye. No one did. They just ordered it, made sure all of my favorite toppings were on at least one of the three they ordered, and got my favorite chicken wings added to their usual order. It was such a sweet gesture that I cried.

It's more than what Camden has done for me. He consistently orders from Pizza Hut because it's cheaper, even though I tell him all of the time that I will pay. I'm not destitute. I might not be making a killing from my books, but I make enough.

I shake my head and focus on the words on my screen. I have to get out of my head. If I don't, it's just going to spiral. Camden is a nice guy. It's not fair of me to make him eat from places he doesn't like just because I can't handle the places he does. I just eat something else. It's fine. We still have a good time.

But he gets mad.

I sigh at my demon and push him out of my mind. He did get upset once, but it was fine after a few minutes. He never yelled at me or anything. And he has a right to be upset if he went through the trouble of picking up dinner for us since I'm incapable of leaving my safe space.

Because you're dumb, Mariah. So, so stupid. I bet you'll ruin this with Camden, the demon tells me.

No. I won't. Camden likes me. He's a good guy. We're seeing how this plays out.

You're a fool. Kieran and Lyric were right. Camden isn't in your league. You're so far below his, you should be grateful that he even looks at you.

"Hey, you okay, Mariah?" Lyric asks softly.

I open my eyes. I didn't know I closed them. I wipe at them when I feel they're wet and shake my head with a sniffle. Kieran and Lyric have pulled Lyric's pool chair close to mine and are sitting on it together. Kieran's leg is against mine. His hand is on my knee. Lyric's hand is on my thigh.

I nod and sniffle, pushing away all of my thoughts. But they're still there fighting to reach the surface. I feel them. They're never quiet. Even when they trick me into thinking they are. I can still hear them. Hear my demon.

"I just..." I trail off. "Um... I think maybe I just need to be alone." I lower my head. I don't want to be. When I'm alone, the demon is louder. Harder to ignore.

"You know that's not happening," Lyric says softly. They both squeeze my leg. It's another thing I love about them. Lyric has anxiety, too. They both know the signs of an attack or an impending one.

"I -" I cut myself off with wide eyes as a wall of water comes at me. Before I can react, the wave of pool water lands directly on me, Lyric, and Kieran, soaking us all. "Ah!" I scream.

Camden's friends are all laughing as he glares dangerously at Kieran. He pulls himself out of the pool as another wave of water comes at us. I move to the side to dodge it, but it lands on me just as much as it does the targets of the intended attack, soaking me and my laptop even more.

The laptop's screen flashes and goes black. My heart starts racing. I push my hair out of my face, taking deep breaths. I keep it on my lap and grab my towel to try and get the water off it. But seconds later, it crackles and sparks starting on fire. Which I wouldn't have known if the bottom didn't suddenly get so hot that it burns to hold.

I quickly stand and toss the smoking laptop on the chair. "Ah!" I scream again.

"Oh my God! Mariah!" Kieran wraps his arms around me and pulls Lyric to us both so they're surrounding me.

"Dude! Get the fuck off her!" Camden yells, ripping Kieran and Lyric away from me.

I fall to the ground in the sudden pandemonium as all of Camden's friends jump out of the pool and surround Kieran, Lyric, and Camden himself. I land hard on my hands and knees. My wrist snaps. Immediate agony flows through my entire left arm.

"Ow!" I instantly fall face first and curl into a fetal position, holding my wrist against my body. Suddenly, Camden grabs my arm, the one I'm cradling, and yanks me up. "Ah! Camden!" Pain shoots through me.

"Fuck, Mariah. Why the hell do you have to allow this motherfucker to touch you?" Camden's dull eyes are suddenly on fire. "Don't you understand you're mine? I don't fucking share!"

"Don't touch her!" Lyric shrieks. She shoves Camden away from me so hard that he staggers back and right into the pool. At the last second, though, he reaches out and yanks Lyric with him.

But my attention is no longer on the chaos unfolding in front of me. It's on the smoke I smell.

Fire! I can feel my demon jumping up and down like he's relishing in my fear.

"Fire," I murmur to myself. My eyes lock onto the flames. My laptop has ignited the pool chair. Part of me is trying to figure out how. The other part of me is screaming to run.

He's gonna get you, my demon laughs. *You're gonna die in a fire. It's your worst fear. It's gonna eat you alive. Burn you.*

The fear wins out.

I spin on my heels and run.

I can feel the heat. The flames. It's chasing me. I know it is. I don't dare look back because it will engulf me. I vaguely hear someone screaming for me, but I don't dare stop.

I won't.

I rip the door open to the apartment building, ignoring the pain shooting through my arm, and sprint up the stairs.

Don't stop! Don't stop! The demon laughs and taunts me. *You look pathetic when you run. Running from a pool chair on fire? Leaving all your shit there? Stupid girl.* He laughs again. *They were all right about you. Camden deserves so much better.*

I cover my ears as I run up the stairs. "Leave me alone!" I tear through the door that leads to my floor and sprint down the hall. I pass a couple of people in a blur as I dash to my apartment.

Never being more thankful that I carry my key on a chain around my neck, I'm terrified of being locked out of my apartment when I go down to the pool, I unlock my door. I fly into my apartment and slam it behind me, quickly locking it.

My eyes dart around my apartment.

I'm gasping for air.

My heart is racing so fast it sounds like a fleet of fighter jets taking off.

"Holy shit," I whisper, gripping my heart. "Holy shit." I sit down in the center of my living room and hug my knees to my chest. I squeeze my eyes shut.

Stupid girl. My demon laughs. *You really showed your crazy this time.*

I shake my head. "No, no, no…"

Yes, yes, yes. You know Camden is running far away from you. He's not going to want to be with a crazy girl like you. And his compliment about you in this bikini? No way he meant that. You're fat. Disgusting. You have stretch marks all over you. You stay inside your apartment all day because you're too afraid to leave these walls.

"No… no… no…"

Camden is done with you. Kieran and Lyric were right. He's so much better than you. You know they don't even like you. They just tolerate you. Just like everyone else.

I cover my ears again. "No… You're lying."

You lost him. You lost them all. Matt and DJ. Lyric and Kieran. Camden. All of his friends. They're gone. They're going to realize what a whiny, unstable, fat little bitch you are!

"No! You're lying!"

"Mariah? Baby, open the door!"

"Camden...," I whisper with wide eyes. My head snaps to the door as he knocks on it. Hard. "Camden!"

Don't get excited now. He's here to tell you he can't handle your crazy.

I shake my head as I crawl to the door. "You're lying!"

"Baby, who's lying? Open the door!" He knocks harder as he jiggles the door handle. "Mariah! Open the door!"

I scramble faster towards the door. I need him. I need him to hold me. Get me out of this blackness trying to envelope me. I unlock the door quickly as I pull myself up and open the door. Tears stream down my face. I can't catch my breath. My demon is yelling at me. Screaming. Laughing.

I launch myself at Camden and bury my face in his chest. "Make it stop. Please, please make it stop!"

Camden hugs me tightly and close. "I got you. I got you, Mariah," he whispers soothingly.

"Hey! Get away from her!" someone yells. I jump, startled, and look towards the voice of some man I don't recognize. "We all saw what happened! The police are on the way!"

My heart skyrockets into a whole other stratosphere.

You see that? They called the police on you because you started a fire. Stupid girl.

I grip Camden as several people rip him away from me. "No!" I reach for him but someone pulls me back. I fight and struggle as I choke on my sobs. The arms are too strong for me, though, and the lack of oxygen is taking its toll. I start to feel sick. My vision begins to darken.

Are you panicking? Just take a deep breath. Jesus. You do this all the time. It's not the demon this time. The voice belongs to Rodney. *I don't know what you want me to do, Mariah. I can't help you. I don't know what to do.*

"Just hug me!" I plead. "All I've ever wanted you to do is hug me!"

Don't, Mariah. I'm sore.

I sob harder. My vision gets blacker and more blurry. I sink against the person keeping me from Camden as people wrestle him to the ground.

So many people. Where did they all come from?

Stupid girl. They're keeping you for the cops. And now he's getting arrested because he ran after you. This is your fault. The demon is back.

My heart hammers against my ribs.

Is it wrong of me to prefer the demon over Rodney?

"I'm sorry. So, so sorry, Camden. Please don't hate me. Please!" I whimper. I'm losing the battle. My body is fighting against all of the ways I use to keep myself from panicking.

I'm going to end up in the hospital. I feel it. I'm getting weaker and weaker.

"Shh… you're okay. Help is on the way," the man holding me whispers. "You're safe."

His voice is soothing. Calming.

But it's too late.

Why didn't Lyric and Kieran come? I ask myself.

Because they don't like you. Stupid girl, my demon answers. It's something I'm starting to agree with him on. *Take my hand, Mariah. You're safe with me. I've always protected you. You know you're safe with me.*

My body trembles as I close my eyes. Safe. It's all I've ever wanted. To feel safe and loved. Protected. My demon may be vicious as hell, but he's always saved me from the wrath of other people's words. Rodney's insults. His emotional and mental abuse. He's always enveloped me when I fell into his dark world. Soothed me when I was too tired to fight.

Why do I always fight you? I ask him. *You always win.*

Come with me, Mariah. All you have to do is take my hand.

A strange sense of warmth fills me as I do what the demon says. I feel myself being pulled into his darkness. His world. His embrace. His own brand of pain and comfort.

I don't see the fight going on.

I don't hear the noise of my heart.

The chaos ceases to exist as my entire world turns pitch black. I can't see anything now. I can't hear anything.

The world falls away, and all I feel is empty.

Chapter Five

☆ DJ ☆

"You're free to go, Nate," I say as I stand, rubbing my head.

Matt hands Nate his card. "If you can think of anything else, please give us a call. My cellphone number is on the back. I have it on all the time."

Nate takes out his phone after taking the card. After a few moments he holds up his phone, showing us the screen with Matt's phone number programmed into it, and hands the card back. "Probably best if I don't have a cop's card lying around."

I chuckle. "Smart kid."

He smiles as he stands, but the smile falls quickly. "Look. I know I wasn't much help. I wish I knew more, but Shannon hasn't been too forthcoming over the past few weeks. I know she had a boyfriend, but it wasn't me. Even if some wished it was. Shannon and I were happy being friends." He chokes up slightly and swallows hard. "Just... find the person who took her from us. She was an incredible woman with a lot of life and her whole future ahead of her."

I nod. "We'll find him." I glance at Matt before looking back at Nate. "Listen, this stays between us. But we knew you weren't our guy.

You've only proven that with your alibi. Hard to kill someone when you're not even in the same country. But anything you can give us. Anything you hear. Anything seems off. I don't care if it seems so small and minute, tell us. We want to bring her killer to justice and give her peace. We want to give you, her family, and all those close to her as much closure as we can."

"And we apologize for having to haul you in like this. I'd hate stepping off a flight and having the cops waiting for me," Matt says, his voice dripping apology.

"Don't worry about it, Lieutenant. I understand. As soon as I was told what happened, I booked my flight. Unfortunately, it's not as easy as some would think getting here from South Africa."

I smile as we walk him out. Nate, our victim, Shannon's, friend, has been trying to get back to the US from South Africa for weeks. He was even kind enough to show us all of the flights and layovers he had to book. And the hassle the United States gave him in getting back into the US. He was forced to stay in Canada for two weeks just to make sure he didn't have any kind of contagious diseases. Like Malaria or Monkeypox.

To top everything off, when we contacted him and told him we needed to speak to him, he agreed to come back right away. With all of the delays he went through and the many airports, he lost his phone. We thought he was skipping out on us, even though we didn't believe for a second he was the culprit.

We were definitely right. Not only does he have one hell of an alibi, but his DNA doesn't match what we found inside Shannon. He's been cooperative as hell and seems genuinely interested in helping us.

As he reaches the door at the front of our building, he turns back. "Shannon was a good girl. She didn't deserve this. I'd bet all of my family's wealth that it was Camden."

My heart skips a beat. Or maybe it stops altogether. "Camden," I mumble.

"He's the football player. Pissed he didn't make the starting line. He's the one that tells everyone he's fucked every single one of the cheerleaders, and that he's the first-string linebacker."

Matt nods. "Right. I have him on the list. You've given us a few people."

"Camden should be at the top. He's a first-class asshole. I don't think Shannon had contact with him, though. He's the kind of dude she'd

run from. It's why I mentioned him last, but the more I think about it…"
He shrugs as he turns and walks out the door.

I rub my head as I turn. "Camden. How do you feel about him?"

Matt follows. "Is it a coincidence that we know a Camden?"

"I'm trying not to think about that, Matt. I texted Mariah asking Camden's last name. She didn't answer. I'm gonna call her as soon as I get back to my office."

"Squads Fifteen and Twenty-five," dispatch calls over the radio as Matt and I enter my office.

We always turn our radio down when we're interviewing, but the office is quiet. Truthfully, I like the sound of the calls out over the radio. Maybe it's a cop thing, but it's soothing. Especially when I'm alone in my office doing reports or something mundane. I reach down and turn my radio up as I sit down behind my desk. Matt sits in a chair in front of it.

The squads answer as I take out my phone and start dialing Mariah's number, but I stop dead in my tracks when our address comes across the radio.

"What the fuck?" Matt turns up his radio a little and holds it to his ear.

"Female was pulled out of a pool. RP says she's breathing but is still unconscious. He also says a male was beaten down by six other males. Currently unconscious. There's another female involved who has passed out after suffering through a panic attack. RP says she was screaming things that didn't make sense."

Matt and I stare at each other in horror before we both leap up and jump at the door. Matt reaches it first and pulls it open so hard, it slams against the wall. I pull it shut behind me and sprint down the hall after him, still listening to the radio.

"We have medical enroute. RP says the six men involved in the fight took off running. He says four of his friends are with him and are subduing one of the people involved. He says a couple of bystanders are by the pool with the woman who was pulled from the pool and the man who was beaten down. One of them is a doctor. My partner has him on the line. RP says the woman he's with is barely breathing. My other partner is talking him through CPR. His friends are fighting with the other male involved."

I whip out my radio as Matt and I jump in my squad. With a squeal of tires, I fly out of the parking garage, lights and sirens blaring. "Squad Four to radio, put me and Twenty-Seven on that call." I glide effortlessly into traffic and speed towards home. Matt puts his hand on the dash and grabs my radio so I can drive with both hands.

"10-4. Four and Twenty-Seven added to the fight call."

"Squad Fifteen to radio. Put me and Twenty-Five two-three."

Matt breathes a sigh of relief as he pulls up the call on the laptop. The laptop will give us more information than what came out over the radio. Things like the apartment number and name of the RP, or responding party.

"Fuck. Mariah's apartment," he says, confirming what we already knew in our hearts. He brings the radio to his lips as I speed through the streets, dodging traffic. "Twenty-Seven to Fifteen and Twenty-Five."

"Go ahead, Lieutenant," one of them says. I don't care which.

"The apartment this is going down in is Mariah Carter's. She has severe anxiety and panic attacks induced by PTSD. The two by the pool are more than likely Lyric Sharpe and Kieran Lockwood. Twenty-Seven to radio, get me more squads. We need to find these other people. I need canvassing done."

"10-4," dispatch responds.

I fly into the parking lot, skidding to a stop behind the other squads. Matt tosses me my radio as we get out of the squad. I key the mic. "Squad Four and Twenty-Seven are two-three. Get me those other squads. Code Three. Where's medical?"

"10-4, Squad Four. ETA on medical is three minutes."

"10-4," I say. Matt and I meet our partners at the front door.

"You two check on the victims by the pool. Straight through the gym. Out the emergency exit. Alarm will sound. I don't give a shit," Matt commands. "Listen for medical. One of you will need to lead them through. Prop the emergency door, so you can get back in."

"Got it, Lieutenant." They both take off running.

"Fucking hell," I rumble as we both start jogging up the stairs to our floor. "I don't like the sounds of any of this."

"You and me both, baby."

We burst through the door onto our floor only slightly out of breath, more from the speed of the climb than the exertion. Matt and I are both in incredible shape. We sprint down the hall towards Mariah's apartment.

"Captain, we have two victims down here. Both breathing but unconscious and in bad shape," one of my officers says.

"10-4. Four to radio, get me another ambulance rolling."

"10-4."

The RP wasn't kidding when he said this guy was fighting. Three of the four guys holding him have an injury of some sort. Black eye. Bloody nose. Fat lip. Scratches. They have him face down on the ground, but he's bucking like a bronco under them.

"Get the motherfucking fuck off me!" he screams. I know that voice.

"Camden," I growl.

Matt launches into the fray of things. "Hands behind your back!"

"Fuck you! Get off me!" Camden flails his arms erratically.

I kneel next to Matt and grab one of Camden's wrists. I twist his arm back so I have complete control of him. I bend his wrist. "Hand behind your back, Camden! Do it now!"

"Ah! Let me fucking go!" he screams.

I bend his wrist a little more. "Now!"

"It's there! It's there! Fuck, let go! Let go!"

I glance at Matt, keeping Camden's arm in my control. Matt snaps a cuff on Camden's other wrist. I move Camden's arm around, keeping control of his wrist. Matt grabs his arm and snaps the cuff on his other wrist.

The entire time we fought with him, our eyes have never left Mariah. Someone is giving her CPR, but she looks pale as fuck and isn't coming to. I look up as more officers come running down the hall with two paramedics and a stretcher with them.

"Thank fucking God," Matt whispers. We both stand, hauling Camden up with us.

"Take him until we figure out what the fuck is going on," I command.

"Yes, sir." One of the other officers takes Camden's arm. He's still fighting and screaming shit about just being up here because of his girl. Demanding to know if she's okay. Like he fucking gives one single shit about her.

Matt and I follow the paramedics into Mariah's apartment. Matt is visibly fighting for some semblance of control. It's not easy for either of us to see Mariah in this state. She told us she's been hospitalized for panic attacks in the past. We both hoped it would never happen again.

I take Matt's arm. "Baby," I say quietly and nod my head towards the kitchen. "Let me talk and interview. Go with her."

His brown eyes widen and water. "What about -"

I shake my head. "Don't. I'm the Captain. This is my scene. I want to go, but you know one of us needs to stay. You go. Kieran and Lyric are involved. I don't have names, but my instincts are telling me it's them. Someone needs to be with her. You're not in the frame of mind to run this scene, baby."

Matt takes a shaky breath and nods. He's a good cop. He's always been able to command the worst of scenes; lead the most horrific of missions. But I can tell when he's hit his limit. This is it. We both have grown to care deeply for Mariah. Seeing her like this is hard for us both, but we need to gather information. I'm the one in the frame of mind to do that. Matt would do the same for me, if the roles were reversed.

The paramedics start working on Mariah. Matt kneels down next to them, ready to help in whatever way they need him to. I take a deep breath and close my eyes. It's one of the quickest ways for me to get myself into Captain mode.

After a moment, I open them. I move aside with the one person who was helping Mariah. He's sitting on the couch with his head between his legs. I sit next to him. He's breathing deeply with his hands locked behind his head. I'm sure that entire thing had to be scary for him.

"Doing at least a little okay? I'm sure this whole thing is a bit fucked up for you."

"Dude. You have no clue," he mumbles. He's young.

I nod in understanding. "How about we start with your name?"

"Austin."

"Austin. Can you tell me what happened?" I take out my small notepad as he nods and sits up.

"We were coming back from class. We thought we'd hit the pool. So, we all headed to our rooms or apartments. We changed quick. We'd decided we'd just meet by the pool. Me and my roommate got out before anyone else. We heard someone scream. We saw her." He nods towards

Mariah. "She jumped up and screamed again. She threw her laptop. By that time, the others had joined us. We were walking kind of slow." He looks at me. "Kind of observing, you know?"

"Understood."

"Well, I don't know what exactly happened to make her throw her laptop and scream, but she did. It must have shocked her or something because after she threw it, the pool chair started on fire."

"Oh, shit." I don't tell him that Mariah has an overwhelming fear of fire, but I file that away for me and Matt for later. It explains a lot. I don't need to see Matt to know he's listening and heard that. We'll talk more later about what he was able to hear and actually process. His attention is more on Mariah. "What happened after that?"

"They were all fighting and screaming. There was a group of guys in the pool, and they all got out. There was another girl who got into the middle of it all, but it looked like she was protecting the girl." He nods again to Mariah.

"Mariah," I say with a nod.

He nods. "I didn't know her name. Anyway, the other girl seemed to be protecting Mariah. The guy who y'all arrested was trying to grab Mariah, but the girl and another guy were pushing him away. I couldn't hear the whole conversation, but the other girl pushed him back hard. He fell in the pool but he grabbed her. Mariah ran. She had no idea what happened next. The guy's friends were all fighting the other dude that I think was a friend of Mariah's. It was like six on one. He had no chance. My friends and I jumped into help. They all took off, but the one that pulled the girl in the pool got out and took off running after Mariah. But the girl…" He trails off.

I wait a few moments before I clear my throat. "What about the girl?"

He sighs and rubs his head as he leans back and closes his eyes. "I saw that she hit her head on the side of the pool when that fucker pulled her in. The way her body jerked as she fell, it didn't look accidental." He shakes his head and opens his eyes. "I didn't realize it at the time, but she was fucking out, man." He looks at me. "A few others had heard and seen what was going on. One of them jumped in after her. She was sinking under the water. Asshole didn't do anything. He just let her sink. It's the reason I ran after him. With everyone else down there helping the guy and girl, my friends followed me. There was a lot of screaming and yelling. Someone was yelling about calling the cops on us. I didn't care. After what he did to her, I didn't know what he planned for Mariah. When we took off, the girl was being pulled out of the pool."

I nod. "So, she hit her head and the guy left her to drown."

"Yes, sir. He got out with a damn smirk on his face. I've seen him and his friends around campus a few times, but I don't know who he is. All I know is he's been in trouble with the school before. He used to be in one of my classes at the beginning of the semester, but he disappeared one day. I heard it was because he'd been kicked out for cheating on a test and was on academic probation. I don't really know if that's the truth."

I write a few things down in my notes. "Anything else you can tell me? Names of those involved? Where they went? Do you know where they live? What apartment?"

"The ones who took off?" He shakes his head. "No clue. But I can identify them if you put them in front of me. It all happened pretty fast, but I'll never forget those faces. Fuck. They were just filled with hatred. Rage. Anger. I can't even describe it. It was fucking terrible to see that. When we jumped in, they kept kicking that guy. One of them spit on him. Then they started fighting us. It wasn't until more people showed up that everyone took off."

"Austin, I appreciate the time. Just need a bit more information from you, then you're free to go."

"Sure. Anything." He leans forward and looks at Mariah. The paramedics have loaded her on the stretcher. I can't tell if she's awake, but by the way Matt's shoulders are hunched over, I could take a guess and probably be right. "Is she gonna be okay?" Austin asks me, not taking his eyes off her.

I swallow because I don't honestly know. "She'll be good." I say the words as much for me as for him.

I stand and follow the other officers out, guiding Austin in front of me. I turn and close Mariah's door when everyone is out and take a breath to steady myself. When I turn again, I force my Captain hat back on and get the rest of the information I need from Austin.

Watching them load Mariah into the back of an ambulance cuts me to the core. Seeing Matt climb in after her holding her hand with his shoulders slouched stabs me in the chest. I can't let those emotions surface right now. I have a lot more time to spend on-scene. Anything I can do to bring this prick to justice, I'll do it.

But when the three ambulances leave the scene, their sirens blaring and a police escort leading them, my heart goes with them. I nearly lose it. It takes every single cell of my being to not jump in my squad and follow them.

"Captain?"

I look over at one of my cops on scene. A Sergeant. A good one. I take another breath, inwardly stealing myself. "Updates for me, Sergeant Ryan?"

He nods. "Yeah. We got a few of the guys involved. We're missing two, according to witnesses. Some recognized them from the baseball team at the university. They gave us apartment numbers, but they aren't there."

I scrub my hands down my face. "Think I'd get fired for busting down a door without a warrant?"

"Uh…" He chuckles. "Probably. But I'm with you. The things I saw and heard are fucked the fuck up."

I let my hands fall to my sides. "The victims. Lyric Sharpe and Kieran Lockwood?"

He raises an eyebrow. "Yeah."

I look down at him. "Call in Captain Sanders."

"I've never known you to give up a case."

"I don't want to. But Lyric and Kieran are friends. Mariah is… something…" I shrug. "Something more, I guess. I hope."

Sergeant Tanner Ryan sucks in a breath and nods. "You know as well as I do that if I go to Captain Sanders, you won't be updated on details."

"Yep. But if I don't pull myself, it's unethical."

Tanner follows my gaze. I'm still watching the ambulances taking away my entire world. They're a lot smaller now. I can only see the lights, but I'm not looking away until I can't see them at all.

After a few moments, he pats me on the back. "Go. I'll run the scene. I'll take the case. I'll advise Sanders, but as far as I'm concerned…" He shrugs and winks before he walks back inside the building, heading to the pool area.

I take him up on his offer without a second thought. I jog to my squad and jump in. I flip on my lights and sirens and tear after the ambulances. I've never left a scene before, but I've never had people I care about involved either.

I don't want Matt dealing with this alone. He needs me as much as I need him. But I also don't want Mariah, Kieran, and Lyric to come out of this without us both there. Lyric and Kieran are like family.

Mariah, though...

I blink back the tears threatening to fall. We should have told her. We shouldn't have stood by and let this thing with Camden go on for as long as it did. Neither of us liked seeing her with another man. We were stupid to not admit our feelings for her.

It doesn't take me long to catch up to the ambulances and the squads escorting them, but the closer we get to the hospital, the more I realize just how right Matt is. We fucked this whole thing up in such an epic way in just a short span of two weeks that I don't know if the damage will ever be able to fixed.

But no fucking way I'm giving up.

Chapter Six

☆ Matt ☆

I pace the small waiting room rubbing my head. DJ is leaning against a wall with his eyes closed. There are several people in this room watching me curiously. DJ and I aren't wearing uniforms, but our guns and badges are clearly visible. I have no doubt in my mind that they probably think we're here for an officer down or something.

It's not something any cop wants to face, and I'm happy it's not one of our guys in this hospital, but this feels worse. I have a family. Lyric and Kieran have become as much a part of me as my actual family. DJ, on the other hand, doesn't. He has my family. They all love him and have accepted him. But Lyric and Kieran to him are sometimes all the family he feels he has. They aren't simply my family who have accepted him that he's come to love back. They're people he's accepted as his family. People he's chosen.

And then we add in Mariah. We both fell for her so quickly, it made our heads spin. And I'm not sure it was in a good way. She threw us so far off our game, neither of us have been thinking clearly. We've wanted to spend all of our time with her. We've wanted to tell her how we felt about her. Unfortunately for us, we're both idiots. It's something I'll be kicking myself over for the rest of my fucking life.

I look up when a doctor slips into the waiting room. He looks around at the several people who all have eyes on him. We're not the only people here waiting for news. Every single person here has someone they care about somewhere in this hospital. We're all looking for any scrap of information we can.

The doctor clears his throat and looks down at his clipboard. He nods and sees my badge. "Lieutenant?"

"Yeah."

He motions me out of the waiting room. DJ and I hurry after him. We all move to the hall, but stay against the wall so we're out of everyone's way. DJ moves just behind me as we face the doctor. He looks through a few pages on his clipboard. I fight the urge to scream at him for anything he has.

Finally, he looks up at me. "You're here for Kieran Lockwood, Lyric Sharpe, and Mariah Carter."

"Yes, sir." I motion to DJ. "We both are."

The doctor nods again. "Mr. Lockwood is awake. Talking. We've run several tests including an MRI. He's okay. He's got some external bruising, but he got away lucky. Usually when someone goes through what he did, we see a lot more internal injuries than we did with him. He has a concussion. He's free to go, but he'll need someone to look out for him for the next twenty-four hours. He looks worse than he is, I assure you."

"Okay. Done. He can stay with us," DJ says. His hand finds my lower back. He rubs it soothingly, helping me to settle.

"He's just signing his discharge paperwork. He said he's not leaving without his girlfriend. Which leads me to Ms. Sharpe." He flips to the next page on his clipboard. "Ms. Sharpe did wake up, but she was screaming and fighting, which sent her into stroke territory. We were forced to put her into a medically induced coma just to keep her from having one. She did, unfortunately, go into cardiac arrest. It was minor, and we were able to stop damage with the medically induced coma, but we'll be keeping her in the sedated state for a few days at the very least while we survey the damage. It's possible she'll end up with a surgery, depending on what kind of issues her cardiac arrest caused. We also believe that she may have had a small stroke when she was underwater. It's just too soon to give much information on that until we're able to run the tests we need to."

"Witnesses say she hit her head after she pulled into the pool," DJ says. Thank fuck for him being able to ask questions and give information. I'm about to pass out.

"We were able to run an MRI after we got her sedated. I can tell you that the head injury wasn't severe enough to cause brain damage, but I don't know yet what kind of damage, if any, the stroke caused. I need to run further tests on her. I don't think any long-term damage occurred. I think Ms. Sharpe will make a full recovery, but I can't make promises on that until I have the tests to back me up."

"Lyric!" a deep male voice reverberates through the emergency room.

"Sir! You can't be back here!" a nurse shrieks.

I look over the doctor's head as DJ moves to my side, still keeping his hand on my back. "Oh. Holy shit, it's Luca," I say with wide eyes.

"Lyric! Where the fuck is my sister?" Luca shoots a withering glare at the nurse trying to grab his arm.

I jump into action and jog down the short corridor to the nurse's desk. "Luca!"

His glare meets my eyes. He immediately softens when he sees it's me. "Fuck, Matt. Where's Lyric? I got your call that she's here!"

Luca Sharpe is Lyric's older brother. He moved to the United States with Lyric from the United Kingdom to escape the completely horrible life Lyric led there. And none of it being her fault. She wasn't into drugs or drinking or prostitution. Nothing at all like that. Lyric is a good girl who was dealt a terrible fucking hand in life. The United States offered her a new start and new life away from the bullshit that she was put through there.

I take his arm and guide him back to where DJ still has the doctor. They're both watching us. "I got him. I was expecting him and forgot to inform the desk," I tell the nurse, using my law enforcement privileges to my advantage. She nods as I guide Luca away. "Fucking hell, Luca. You should have called me. I thought you were in Seattle on a job. It's why I left the message saying to call."

"I came home early. I got in yesterday. I was going to surprise Lyric tonight. Kieran and I had a whole plan. What the hell is going on?"

I quickly fill him in as we walk back, giving him the cliff notes version and telling him what the doctor told us. Luca rubs his head as he leans against the wall near the waiting room.

"We were just about to hear about what happened to Mariah," DJ says.

The doctor glances down at his clipboard. "Ms. Carter. She's physically okay. She has a twisted wrist. We didn't splint or even brace it because she said it's feeling better. We'd like to keep her for a few days. She doesn't qualify for a fifty-one-fifty, but we still want to observe her. When she came in, she was conscious and screaming things that simply did not make sense. But she wasn't threatening harm to herself or anyone. After we got her calmed, she said she's not suicidal. She admitted to an almost attempt when she was seventeen, but she hasn't been in that mental state since. That's been twenty-three years. The issue is she doesn't want to stay."

I feel my heart breaking even more. I pinch the bridge of my nose and close my eyes. A fifty-one-fifty is a forced seventy-two-hour psychiatric hold. I let out a breath. "She spent five days in a hospital when she was a teenager. In and out of consciousness. It was caused by a panic attack. Since then, she's been in twice more. Every single time, she was alone."

I hear a strangled sob covered by a cough escape DJ's throat as I open my eyes. "She won't be this time," he says. "We'll stay with her."

The doctor lets out a sigh and nods. "I'll move Mariah and Lyric to the same room. I assume Mr. Lockwood won't be leaving either."

I shake my head. "Not without Lyric. And neither will Luca." I nod to him.

"I can do a private suite, but their insurance -"

"Do it," Luca commands before Matt or I can. "I don't care what it costs. I'll figure out a way to pay it. But none of us are leaving."

"We," I say. "We'll figure out a way to pay it." I meet Luca's eyes. He nods, understanding that we're all in this together.

The doctor tucks his clipboard under his arm. "I'll put in the order and let you know the room. If anyone asks, I'm doing it on the orders of the Gainesville Police Department." He looks up at us all. We nod our agreement. "I have orders in for further tests on Lyric." He looks down at the floor before looking back up at me. I'm taller than he is by a foot. He's not a big guy. "Ms. Carter wants to leave AMA."

"We'll take care of it," DJ chokes out. I know he's about to break. The doctor leaves with a nod after giving us her current room number here in the ER as I turn and hug DJ. His arms come around my waist, and he hugs me hard. "We did this, Matt. This never would have happened if we'd just told her."

I don't have the ability to argue with him because I wholeheartedly agree. The only difference between my feelings and his is that I don't think it's *our* fault. I don't think *we* did this. This isn't on DJ at all.

It's on *me*.

(Two Days Later)

"Mmm…"

My eyes flutter open, and I yawn. It takes me a little while to realize where I am.

The hospital.

A private room.

I lift my head with another yawn as DJ shifts. I realize my head had been nestled in his lap on his dick. It's one of my favorite positions to rest when I need to but can't actually be in bed. DJ is soothing.

"Mmm…"

I squeeze DJ's thigh and shift, my head snapping to the beds. Lyric and Mariah were put in the same room. Luca is sleeping in a chair with his feet up on Lyric's bed. Kieran is holding her tight and close. He's in her bed with her.

DJ and I have a small cot set next to Mariah. He's sitting up with his back propped against the wall looking at both girls. Neither of us got much sleep the past couple of days. Both of us finally dozed off a little while ago.

"I think she's having a nightmare," Kieran says quietly. "I've been watching her a little." He buries his face in Lyric's hair and closes his eyes as he sniffles.

Lyric has yet to wake up, but she is stable. She has no severe injuries. No serious damage. Her brain function appears to be working perfectly, at least per all the tests and shit they've run on her. I guess we won't really know everything until she wakes up.

"Mmm…"

I drag my eyes from Lyric. I hate how frail and pale she looks. It's heartbreaking on so many levels, but probably the most because Lyric is like mine and DJ's little sister. We know how strong and vibrant she is. Seeing her in this state kills us. None of her family has called, though they all know. All she has here is us, Kieran, and Luca. It shouldn't surprise, but it does. I don't understand how anyone can be aware one of their relatives is in this state and not even check in. I'd never be able to be so callous.

I shift and sit up. The move causes DJ to groan as he opens his eyes. Mariah sniffles in her sleep and jerks her head to the side. Her hand twitches. Her eyes are darting back and forth behind her closed eyelids.

"Jesus," I say as I move to her side.

"Mariah?" DJ rumbles, blinking himself awake.

I sit next to her and pull her into me so she's sitting. I wrap my arms around her. "Shh… I got you, baby," I whisper in her ear, pulling her into my chest. She's not hooked up to machines or an IV. It's much easier to pull her into me this way.

She trembles and jerks into me. "Mmm…" It's a moan that would typically be peaceful, but it's anything but right now. It's barely above a whisper, but she's struggling. It sounds like she wants to scream but can't.

DJ sits behind her and wraps his arms around both of us. He presses his lips against her neck as we both sway gently with her, holding her close and tight between us. Her small hand bunches my t-shirt into her fist. I feel her tears before I realize they're falling.

"Shh… We got you, sweet girl," DJ rumbles against her neck. "No one is going to hurt you, baby."

We convinced Mariah to stay in the hospital, as the doctor suggested, but we had to promise that we wouldn't leave her side. She didn't want to be alone. She was scared. She still is. Every time she wakes up, she looks at all of us and says she didn't think we'd be here when she opened her eyes.

DJ kisses me over Mariah's shoulder as we keep gently swaying from side to side. I close my eyes and let him bring me the comfort I desperately need. We get that in different ways. For me, he gives it to me. Gentle kisses. Touches to let me know he's with me. Allowing me to lie on his lap while he rubs my back.

It's different for him. Sometimes, he needs a hug or touch. He loves the sweet kiss. Even a look relaxes him at times. But what really brings him the comfort he needs is making sure I'm okay. That everyone around him is. Only then is DJ actually truly content.

We're both dominant, Alpha males. We have to be in order to hold the jobs and positions we do. We're both nurturers. We want to make sure that those around us are okay. Sometimes, we forget that we need to be okay, too. Luckily for us, we have each other to keep us grounded and healthy when our minds are on everyone around us.

DJ pulls away from the kiss gently. I smile weakly. As it always does, the kiss sends jolts through my entire body. I feel like my blood is electrified. Like it's humming through my being. My dick is instantly hard and begging for relief. It doesn't matter if the time is appropriate or not. My attraction to him has never lessened over the years. I always want him.

Just like Mariah. Every time she looks at me, I feel like she sets me ablaze with need and desire. As it does with DJ, my entire body reacts to her, and it doesn't matter if the time is right. I know with more certainty every single day that these two incredible people are the loves of my life.

I breathe in Mariah and kiss her neck as she starts to calm. I don't look towards the door when it opens. Nurses and doctors are in and out of here all day long. I've become completely numb to all of them.

I sigh and glance up when someone stops next to Mariah. I grip her tighter when I don't recognize the guy. He's not wearing a doctor's coat. He's in jeans and a button-down black shirt untucked. I raise an eyebrow at the sneakers.

"Can we help you?" DJ asks with a glare, not letting either of us go as he looks at the dude.

"You must be DJ and Matt," the guy says.

I look up at him when he says our names. I furrow my eyebrows. "And you are?"

"My apologies. I'm Wyatt Kyle. I'm Mariah's psychologist." He holds out a hand for us to shake. We share a look with each other and shake his hand. Mariah grips my shirt tighter. He smiles. The guy is young.

He has to be in his twenties. His hair is short. It looks like he just rolled out of bed and looks as good as he does.

"You look young to be a psychologist," DJ says with a half-smile, voicing my thoughts exactly.

Wyatt grins. "Yeah, I'm almost thirty. Mariah is one of my first clients."

"He's really good," Mariah whispers with a sniffle. I kiss her shoulder and rub my hands up and down her back. Keeping her grip on my shirt, she looks up at Wyatt. Her face is streaked with tears. "What are you doing here?" she whispers as she looks down. "They said you were on vacation."

Wyatt smiles and takes a folding chair near the wall. He puts it down next to Mariah and sits. "I got back a couple days ago. My first day back was today. I got an urgent message from your doctor about you being here. I contacted him this morning. He told me you're doing okay, but wanted me to visit if I could. Truth be told, I would have anyway."

Mariah takes a breath and nods. "I... never... wanted... to be here... Ever again."

Wyatt nods. "It's scary, huh? Brings back a lot of memories we haven't had an opportunity to work through yet."

Mariah nods again. "And Lyric..."

Wyatt looks over his shoulder then back at Mariah, who still hasn't met his eyes. My heart breaks all over again. "I was briefed a little bit about what happened," Wyatt says gently.

Mariah wipes her eyes. "I don't even know what happened," she whispers.

"We've told her," I say quietly as I run my fingers through her hair. "She's been struggling to really grasp it all. She's been fighting quite a bit to process everything."

"I... just... can't really comprehend it." She bites her lip. I run my thumb over it as DJ presses against her back and kisses her shoulder. Mariah sniffles. "I put it together in pieces. But then my demon doesn't let me accept it. He says everyone is lying."

Wyatt nods. "He's trying all his old tricks again. Making you feel like you're crazy to believe anyone but him." He glances at me and DJ before looking back at Mariah. "Before we continue, are you okay with them being in here? We can go somewhere quiet and private if you prefer."

Mariah meets his eyes for the first time and nods slowly. "I would like them to stay," she says softly. We both give a quiet, relieved sigh. Mariah takes a deep breath. "He keeps saying that I need to just give all of this up and give into the inevitable. I should be alone and stay alone. And I should listen to him because he's never led me astray. He's protected me from the evils of the world."

I inhale sharply but quietly. DJ's eyes widen. We've heard about what Mariah calls a demon that lives in her mind. That voice telling her she's not good enough, pretty enough, or strong enough. The one that tells her she's a burden. But we've never been privy to the extent of the torture she endures.

Wyatt shakes his head. "But we know he's lying to you, don't we? Because we know that's not what's best for you. We know that you took a chance with Matt and DJ. You opened up to them, at least some, and they led you to Lyric and Kieran. When we met last week before my weekend away, you told me that things were going great with them. You still questioned their intentions and motives, but things were going well."

As the two of them talk, I give into myself and hug Mariah tighter. I bury my face in her hair and let DJ sway gently with us both as we quietly listen. I feel like all either of us can do right now is offer her comfort while her therapist helps her make sense of everything happening.

Hopefully, DJ and I can pick up on things he does so we can implement as much as we can into our daily life with her. I don't know what's going to happen or what to do right now, but I know one thing for abso-fucking-lutely certain.

Mariah belongs with us.

There's no fucking way either of us are letting her fight alone.

Chapter Seven

✰ Mariah ✰

(Three Days Later)

"So, wait a second," DJ growls. I look up at him as he starts rubbing his head. His tone has changed. When he answered the phone, he seemed to be happy. Now, his eyebrows are furrowed together, and he's rubbing his temples like he has a headache. "Fuck, come on. Even with the witnesses? How the fuck is this possible?"

It doesn't take much for me to realize that he's talking about Camden. After I spoke with my psychologist in the hospital, I had what they called a mental breakthrough. It caused my hospital stay to be extended by two days, but even I'll admit it was worth it. That I was where I needed to be as so much shit flooded back.

I sit up and rub my own head. I'd been laying in DJ's lap just relaxing with him today. Matt went into work. Neither of them have been there in a week because they've been in the hospital with me and Lyric. When I was released, they came home with me. Luca and Kieran stayed with Lyric, who still hasn't woken up.

It's your fault. She's hurt because of you.

I put my head in my hands and sniffle. *I know.*

"Then we'll build a strong fucking air-tight case," DJ growls. "We'll see you when you're home, baby. Dinner is almost done." DJ pauses and leans forward. He starts rubbing my back soothingly. "I love you, too." He hangs up the phone and wraps an arm around me, pulling me close. "I don't know what he just said to you, baby, but it's not true."

I nod and let him pull me with him as he leans back against the couch. I snuggle into him and let him calm me. I'm not sure what he and Matt do, but my demon is quieter when they're around. Sometimes, I can hear his voice, but mostly, he doesn't come out. He leaves me be.

I've fought him since I was a young child. Maybe only ten or so. He didn't show up until around then, even though most of the trauma I endured happened before that. The older I got, the more the anxiety and depression kicked in. The more the PTSD reared its ugly head. The more the demon made himself more prevalent.

My life hasn't been easy since. I portrayed that I was just fine on the outside. No one knew I was being torn to shreds on the inside. No one saw the scars. No one knew I preferred the company of my bedroom over the company of literally anyone else. To this day, no one has a clue what goes on inside me.

Well, not no one. I opened up to Lyric and Kieran. Lyric has a lot of the same issues I have. It was nice to be able to talk to someone who truly understood me and what I was saying. Kieran, Matt, Luca, and DJ are all very good at understanding it all, too. Probably because they have experience with Lyric.

"I should probably check the chicken," I say quietly.

DJ kisses the top of my head. I have to fight the moan threatening to escape as I get up and walk to the kitchen. When I woke up in the hospital, the only thing I could think of was that I didn't want to be there. I didn't want to be alone. I didn't want to fight by myself. I wanted to just give up completely.

Matt and DJ refused to allow that. I kept thinking of Camden and how I needed to call him. How he should be there. I'd completely blocked out everything that happened at the pool that day. The way his grip on my arm hurt me. How he made me feel like my panic was stupid. How I was stupid for experiencing it. I kept telling myself that I overreacted because of the fire. I knew I didn't, but my mind wouldn't allow me to think otherwise. The demon wouldn't let me see the truth. Matt and DJ would tell me all they found out, and the demon would talk me totally out of listening to all they said.

The truth is, according to witnesses who saw what was happening, Camden caused Lyric's injuries. She may have accidentally hit her head on the side of the pool, but he left her to drown after the hit rendered her unconscious. He got out of the pool and came after me while his friends beat the shit out of Kieran. Witnesses saw that. Someone had to dive into the pool to save Lyric.

And I ran away.

Just like I always do.

So, so selfish of you. No one knows if she'll wake up now. You killed her.

I drop the pan I took out of the oven on top of the stove and close my eyes just as Matt walks into my apartment. I hear the door open and see him out of the corner of my eye before I squeeze them shut. He drops his gear and comes straight to my side.

"Hey," he whispers as he wraps his arms around me. Moments later, DJ joins in the hug. "What's that fucker saying to you, baby? It's not true. You know it isn't." They both sway with me.

I take a deep breath and inhale their scents. Matt is spicy. Masculine. Strong. Woodsy, but not overpowering. It's like being welcomed home. DJ is fresh. Calm. Relaxing. Like a walk through the woods on a rainy day. That refreshing and powerful scent. Inhaling them cuts through the bullshit in my head. Suddenly, the world is right again.

I pull back slowly, not really wanting to. I clear my throat. "Dinner is done," I say quietly with a soft smile.

Matt kisses me softly right on the lips. I melt. Both DJ and Matt have been doing things like that more often. They've told me it's because they're showing me through their actions that they want to be more than friends. It was something I didn't think possible. How could someone like me be wanted by just one of them? Let alone both? I don't feel like I'll ever measure up to the standards they deserve.

But it doesn't seem to matter to them. I've always known they're together. They have been for many years. But they never got married to each other because they wanted to wait for the one special someone they knew belonged with them. They believe it's me.

Me.

My heart really wants to believe that. But I'm a prisoner of my own mind. My demon keeps reminding me that I felt Camden was out of my league, too. And he proved me right. DJ and Matt told me what Lyric overheard the morning she…

I can't even think the words without choking up. Lyric is in a coma right now. And here I am feeling sorry for myself and thinking of two hot guys and their true intentions with me. I'm thinking of how much I want them both, and she's fighting for her life.

I blink away the tears and start dishing up dinner. Chicken and rice. It's my favorite comfort food. Simple, yet incredible. White rice with Cream of Mushroom soup. Some seasoning. And some chicken thighs or quarters. Then it just goes in the oven for an hour and comes out delicious.

"Don't think we're letting this go, baby," DJ rumbles against my neck right before he kisses it. "Just because that smells extremely enticing doesn't mean either of us didn't notice the way you're fighting back tears."

"Or that I forgot you didn't answer me when I asked you what that demon is filling your head with."

They both are far too intuitive. They have a habit of getting right into the thick of the root causes of issues that I don't even understand. They haven't left my side since I was admitted to the hospital. They've stayed with me in my apartment. They've snuggled me in my bed so I didn't have to sleep alone. They've proven their words with their actions.

But the truth is, I fall easily and fast. Hard. And that terrifies me. I've been hurt by every single person I've fallen for. They're already in control of my heart. With every single move they make, it shakes the entire foundation I stand on, which is already cracked. I'm easy to break. After all these years of being treated awfully by those close to me, those supposed to protect me and love me, I'm not sure I can handle another cut. I don't think I'd heal from it this time.

Therein lies the entire issue I face. I believe what they say. At least my heart does. But I've learned not to trust my heart. My heart is stupid. I only have to point to Camden to prove that. And then to Rodney. My way too many years relationship with a man who probably loved me at some point, maybe still does, but was never capable of showing it in ways I deserved. Someone who simply couldn't comprehend that the way he spoke to me was wrong.

I could keep going and point to Bevan. A five-year relationship with an asshole who lost his temper more than he ever tried to have an actual relationship. Or maybe Lewis. The dickhead who was my friend for so many years. I was never good enough for more, but he sure liked the sex.

I sit down with a sigh. Matt and DJ sit down on either side of me, and I almost instantly melt. I'm getting so used to this. I shouldn't be. Things that are seemingly this good never last that long. But being with them is second nature. It's like a natural progression in not only our relationship but in life in general. Like all of my struggles led me to them. The pain. Heartbreak. All endured so I'd appreciate the beauty in them and what they offer.

A love that's true. Respectful. Filled with honesty and compassion. Support. Strength. The kind of love that only comes once in a lifetime. Everything that I never knew existed. That I didn't dare believe existed.

My very own fairytale.

Every fairytale comes to an end, my demon hisses.

Fuck you, I say back to him.

As if they know, Matt and DJ both press closer to me. And just like that, his voice fades into the background. Like noise that gets quieter and quieter the further away it gets. I take a deep breath as we finish eating. DJ takes our plates to the sink. It's all so normal and domesticated. We do everything together so seamlessly.

Matt wraps an arm around me and pulls me close. "So, tell me. What did he say?"

I chuckle and burrow into him. I rest my ear over his heart and hug myself. "That it's my fault Lyric is hurt."

"Well, that's ridiculous. You're not the one who let her sink under that water."

I shrug softly. "No… What I did was worse. I ran."

I look up when I hear DJ's low rumble of warning as he turns around. He leans against the counter and crosses his muscular arms over his chest. "Are you seriously going to sit there and tell me that you're blaming yourself because you got scared? Because I won't agree. Not even a little. You have PTSD, baby girl. You were surrounded by four fucking fires living in the middle of literally nowhere. You had evacuation orders that were to be implemented if the command was given. Mariah, that's scary as fuck to an adult. You were only seventeen. And that doesn't take into account what happened to you when you were a child."

I look down and take a deep breath. He's right. When I lived in Montana, there were three different forest fires around me. One of them was in Idaho, but we always got the smoke from it. Another was on the backside of the mountain range I lived near. It was only around twenty or so miles from where I lived.

The most scary was the third one. It was across from us. It was called the Canyon Ferry Fire. It was the closest. Less than five miles away. The last one was ahead of the Canyon Ferry Fire, but it was burning on the same mountain range. They didn't believe the two would end up combining. I honestly don't remember if it ever did.

Truthfully, I only remember a few things from the entire incident. The first was the smoke. The second was the evacuation order and how quickly we'd need to move if the Canyon Ferry Fire jumped the highway or the one behind us peaked and started moving down the mountain towards us.

And the third was that my dad still delivered people's papers. He delivered in the fire area. At one point, I remember the ground being on fire right next to us. The heat from the flames as he maneuvered through it. How terrified I was hearing the crackling of the flames rolling along the ground. And how pissed I was that he drove in the area in the first place.

It was something I have still, to this day, never forgotten. I'm not even sure I've forgiven my father for that. The fires surrounding us was enough to give me PTSD, but I had it before stemming from what happened to me as a kid. I think Montana is what tipped it over the edge. Now, I can't even light a match. I can't light a fire. And being around one, even a campfire, sends my heart racing.

People think my fear of fire is irrational. They don't understand the repercussions I have to live with after my experiences with it. They don't understand how seeing that pool chair on fire made my mind revert back to a place it hasn't been in years. A dark, dark place. The pool chair fire may never have actually chased me, but I honestly felt like it was. I felt like wherever I went, the fire was surrounding me. I didn't need my demon screaming at me to make me believe it. I already did. I felt the heat. The intensity. I felt the flames licking at my heels as I ran.

Matt lifts my face to his. "Hey. Come back to us." He kisses me softly. His voice is soothing enough to calm me; powerful enough to bring me back.

DJ's arms wrap tightly around me. He kisses the back of my neck. I hadn't even noticed he sat down. "Baby, I will never pretend to understand what goes on in your head, but I won't for a second let you go on believing shit that isn't true," he rumbles against my neck.

I take a deep breath and let myself sink into him. Them. "I feel like I could have done something. Paid more attention. Maybe if I stayed, none of it would have happened. Kieran wouldn't have been beaten up. Lyric -"

Matt shakes his head and tugs my hair gently. "Listen to me, sweet girl. Nothing would have changed. Nothing. Witnesses saw the fight already going down. By the time you started running, people were already jumping into action. Camden slipped away after you only because of the sheer number of people that showed up. It was chaos, and he was easily able to slip away."

DJ kisses my shoulder. "I know it's hard to think about, but if things hadn't happened as they did, the outcome may have ended up worse. So many different scenarios could have occurred. We know about the bet. Lyric told us. And we trust Lyric. We know that when he broke it off after getting what he wanted, it would have devastated you. But we don't know how far that would have gone. We don't know what his further plans were. And it's not something any of us want to think about, baby. I know I sure as hell don't."

I can only nod as the tears start falling. "I just want Lyric to be okay!" I sob into Matt's chest. It's not the first time I've broken down in tears over this. I know it won't be the last.

"We all do, sweet girl. We all do," Matt whispers.

"She's in the best place for her. She's not alone. She has a team of doctors monitoring her. And we know that they're just waiting for her to wake up. We know she doesn't have any severe physical trauma." DJ shifts so he can more fully press against me.

It takes a long while before I finally calm and begin to let their words sink in; before I allow myself to really trust in their actions once more. Ever since this... thing with us started, I've been analyzing and picking apart everything that they do. At the end of the day, though, there's really only one conclusion.

If they didn't care about me, they would never spend as much time with me comforting me and making me feel like my feelings are valid. Matt and DJ have not only made it clear with their words where they stand, but they've also shown me with their actions. And with each word and action, my mind is starting to comprehend that maybe, just maybe, this thing is real.

Maybe they really do like me.

Maybe this thing we have will blossom.

Maybe they'll be the ones to keep my demon away; keep him from dragging me back…

Chapter Eight

☆ DJ ☆

I yawn as I look at the clock on Mariah's nightstand. I rub my eyes and try to figure out why I'm awake at four in the morning.

And then I hear it.

The loud as fuck banging and yelling.

"Mariah! Open the fucking door!" a male voice yells.

I move to get out of the bed, but realize Mariah is wrapped around me. "Fuck," I whisper as the knocking and yelling intensifies. The pill she was given for her anxiety knocks her the hell out. A bomb could drop in this very room. I doubt she'd move an inch.

"Go. I got her. It sounds like Camden," Matt whispers. He tightens his grip on her as I slide my arm out from under her. Matt replaces my arm with his, and she snuggles closer to him in her sleep.

"Mariah! Get the fuck up! Or I'm busting in the fucking door! You fucking owe me!"

"The fuck is going on?" I ask no one in particular. I grab my phone when it starts vibrating. "Christ. What the fuck?" I slip out of the room as Mariah stirs. I hear Matt silencing her soothingly. I answer my phone, barely glancing at the name flashing across the screen. "What?" I growl into the phone.

"Captain?" Tanner asks.

"Yeah?" I reach for the lock on the front door, confident I'm punching Camden the fuck out.

"Mariah! Open the fucking door!" Camden screams.

"Captain, fuck! Are you with Mariah?" Tanner asks. He's out of breath, but something about his voice sends chills down my spine.

I stop with my hand on the lock. "What's going on?"

"Mariah! Open the door!" Camden screams just before he slams his body into it.

"One of the neighbors called. Camden is at Mariah's. He's banging on the door. He's got a fucking gun!"

I immediately back away from the door and sprint back to the bedroom. I close the door, keeping the phone to my ear. "Fuck!" I whisper yell as I rummage through the drawer for my locked gun case. I throw it on the bed and use my phone for light as I put in my combination.

"DJ? The fuck is going on?" Matt launches into action. Mariah stirs but doesn't wake up. He grabs his own gun case and inputs his own combination ready to back me up without any kind of information at all.

The pounding has lessened as I pick my phone back up with my left. My gun is in my right. Matt and I cautiously make our way to the bedroom door. "What's going on, Sergeant?" I ask. He's my eyes on Camden, and he knows it.

"Pulling in now. Dispatch says a couple of his friends pulled him away from the door screaming about how the cops were here. They went down a stairwell."

I glance back at Mariah then Matt. "You stay. I'm going. There's no chance they can cover all exits."

"You're not fucking going without backup, and we can't leave Mariah alone," Matt says darkly.

I know he's right, but it doesn't stop me from wanting to give chase. "Backup is outside." I reach for the doorknob.

Matt puts a hand on my arm. "No. No, DJ. Mariah needs you around. I fucking need you. You know going after him is a fucking suicide mission. He has the advantage."

I narrow my eyes. "Matt, there's no time to argue. He's carrying a fucking gun. And he's pissed. There's no telling what he's capable of." I turn the knob and slip out the door. "Where are you, Ryan?"

"We're setting up a perimeter. No one has come out of the building. There's no way they could've gotten out before we got there. You're on the top floor. Dispatch advised us right away. They're still in the building."

Matt grabs my arm again. I can see the worry written all over him. "DJ, Jesus. Don't. You're not even wearing a vest."

"Cap, I'm advising you to stay in the apartment. Let us do our job. I called SWAT. We'll search. I'm command for SWAT. I'll mobilize. We'll find him."

I sit down in one of Mariah's oversized chairs as Tanner hangs up. My gun is still in my hand. I rest it on the arm of the chair as I close my eyes and swallow. I hadn't realized my heart rate had spiked. I pinch the bridge of my nose. I feel Matt gently take my gun and hear him place it with his on the coffee table behind him.

He drops to his knees in front of me just before I feel his hands grip my thighs tightly. His lips find mine in a hurried yet languid and deep kiss. My hands are instantly on him. All over him. His arms. Hair. Abs. Chest. Back.

Matt, though, is far too good at this. He knows me way too well. He's not going to let me control anything. Not when I feel as out of control as I do. Nope. He's going to make sure I have none of it by leading the pace and slowing me down.

When I try to dominate the kiss, Matt nips my tongue. The shock of his teeth pulls me back. When I grab his cock over his boxer briefs and start rubbing at a furious pace, Matt grabs my hand and holds it against his length.

Matt straddles me, effectively pinning me to the chair. His tongue strokes mine slowly and deeply. The only thing I can think of is how his tongue is stroking the wrong thing. How it should be licking my dick instead. I grip his ass and push him down on my cock. I grind into him.

"You know damn well that isn't how this is going to go down," Matt growls into my neck. "Don't make me take out the cuffs," he whispers against my neck with a grin.

The rumble of his voice shoots jolt after jolt of anticipation down my spine. My already hard length turns to fucking granite at the promise in those words. I contemplate fighting it a little more, but he's already won. The goal was to get my mind off chasing Camden down and fucking killing him with my bare hands. Matt has already succeeded in shifting my focus.

I grin against his lips and open my eyes. I love when he smiles at me with that cocky smirk. It makes me so much harder. And Matt really likes when I'm hard for him. So much so that he tenses. His cock becomes even harder for me.

I squeeze it a little more firmly as I stroke it slowly. "You know how much I love when you get like this for me."

I'm rewarded with that damn cocky smirk. The one that undoes me every fucking time. "Just as much as I love riding you like a bucking bronco. But that's not what you need today."

I raise an eyebrow. "I don't? Because I can assure you, watching you ride me might just be exactly what I need."

He shakes his head and moves off my lap. I almost whimper at the loss of him against me and his dick in my hand, but I know my man. I know he'll make it all worthwhile for us both, even though I won't get a shred of the control I crave. This is his show.

"You might like watching me take that nine-inch, thick dick of yours, but you also love when I suck it." He drops to his knees, not taking those dark and devilish eyes off mine. Not even when he frees my dick and wastes no time taking it in his mouth.

I'd let my head fall back, but I love watching him suck me way too much. "Fuck, Matt. Oh, fuck, baby."

He grins, keeping his eyes on me. His tongue swirls around my tip as he sucks hard. I watch him reach down and start stroking himself. He moans around me and has me damn near coming. I'm that close already. My fingers itch to dive into his hair. Tug. Fuck his mouth.

But that's not how this game is played.

I grip the arms of the chair and watch him stroke my dick and his as his head bobs up and down. He swallows around me and rumbles deeply, sending vibrations through my shaft. My balls are so tight, I'm not sure how they haven't drawn up into my stomach. My abs clench with the effort it takes me to be a good boy and focus all of my attention on Matt. A shiver shoots down my spine straight to my length, but I refuse to come.

Not yet.

Not when his eyes look so hungry. Or when his mouth looks so fucking good sucking my cock. He squeezes my dick a little harder as he strokes the part of my shaft that he can't fit in his mouth. He sucks harder, licks faster, and bobs his head to the rhythm he's jerking himself. He rumbles and swallows around me every time I touch the back of his throat.

"Fuck…, Matt." I finally give in and let my head fall back, closing my eyes. I grip the arms of the chair even tighter and groan.

I can feel him smile around my cock as he rewards me with harder sucks, faster strokes, and lower rumbles. The shivers running down my spine turn into full blown tremors. My dick thickens for him, and I moan gutturally.

"There we go," Matt rumbles around me. "Doesn't that feel better? Letting it all go…" He goes back to sucking and stroking, twisting his wrist. He flicks his tongue over my tip rapidly.

"Oh fuck, Matt. Holy Christ, I'm gonna come."

He grins as I look down. "Come for me, Captain."

I don't need to see my eyes when I look down at him to know they darken. Matt swallows around my dick as I come hard, jerking into his mouth; shooting jet after jet of come down his throat. I barely hold back the roar that wants to escape my mouth. Fuck knows I don't want to wake the beautiful woman soundly sleeping in her bedroom. Not sure I could anyway, but I don't want to chance it.

So instead, I bite my lip and moan as I watch my incredibly sexy Lieutenant swallow every single drop of me that I spurt into his mouth. I don't know how the hell he does it, but he watches me the entire time with a grin on his face as he swallows me like I'm all he needs to survive. He licks me clean and kisses my dick as he stands, still stroking his own cock.

He crooks a finger at me, beckoning me to him. "I'm gonna come so fucking hard, DJ. Suck me."

"Like you need to make that command twice." I lean forward, still following his unspoken rules, and keeping my hands to myself. I take his dick in my mouth with a cocky smirk of my own and look up at him, my eyes just as hungry as his.

Matt tangles his fingers in my hair and pulls me closer. Usually, I'd be doing things to drive him crazy. Like rolling his balls in my hand while I stroke him. Matt knows me very well, though. He knows what he needs to do to get me out of my own head. He's completely aware that this is it. Just like this.

I moan low and suck hard, scraping my teeth along the vein running along his length. Matt thrusts a couple of times before I know it's all he can handle. I close my eyes as he comes, relishing in the taste of the man who owns my heart. I swallow everything he gives me, digging my nails into the fabric of the chair as I lick him clean.

"Well…, that's… not exactly… what I thought I'd see when I came to get a bottle of water," Mariah whispers.

Matt and I turn to look at her. I release his dick from my mouth slowly. She's leaning against the wall with her arms wrapped around her middle like she's hugging herself. She licks her lips, and it's quite obvious her eyes are fixated completely on our dicks. Knowing that, for the first time in our brief relationship, she's both seen Matt and I together in a sexual act, and also seen us fully exposed to her, is a huge turn on.

But the single factor that has us both at full mast instantly is the heat we can see in her eyes, even in low light from across the room. She shifts just enough to subtly cross her legs. To anyone else it would look casual. To us? We know damn well watching us made her wet as fuck.

"You know…," I begin with a smirk, letting my eyes wander up and down her body. She's sinful. And the fact that she only wears a tight tank top to bed and sexy little panties makes resisting her very difficult. "We can help you out with that sudden heat you have spreading between your thighs."

She lets out the most adorable, shocked gasp as her eyes widen. "DJ!"

She uncrosses her legs but keeps them pressed together. Matt growls low as we both watch her. He gives her that sexy cocky smirk and crooks his finger at her. Neither of us have bothered packing ourselves away. There's really no point for what we have planned. Nothing in the world sounds better than making Mariah come as she strokes us.

Given she's to that point, of course. It doesn't matter how much we want her. We've all agreed that we're taking it all at her pace. We know where we are and what we want, but none of it matters if she's not on the same page as us.

Mariah pads softly towards, still hugging herself as she watches us closely. When she reaches us, I stand slowly next to Matt. We both take one of the hands she's tightly gripping herself with. She watches us shyly, but the desire she's radiating is obvious.

We lead her to the couch and sit next to each other. We position her in front of us and look up at her. Matt leans in and kisses her stomach. I kiss between her perfectly supple tits with a low groan. She makes a sexy, quiet whimpering sound that makes my dick twitch.

Matt lets go of her hand and rests his on her hip, squeezing gently. "What do you think, baby? Ready to let us show you just how much we want you?"

She licks her lip. She has no idea how much I want her to say yes, but when she nods slowly, it's all the permission we need. Matt and I both grip the waistband of her panties and pull them down, keeping our eyes on hers, though that's hard as hell, considering I can smell her arousal and want nothing more than to bury my tongue in her smooth as satin pussy.

We lean back with our thighs touching. We pull her down so she's straddling my left leg and Matt's right. Gently, we nudge her legs further apart. She watches us both with curiosity and unbridled passion as she hesitantly uses our shoulders to brace herself.

I smile as Matt and I both grip the hem of her shirt. We slowly start dragging it up as we watch her. "So, pretty," I say raspily.

She blushes. The room is starting to get lighter as the sun starts to rise. I don't know how much time has passed since we woke up, but I don't care. Matt's plan for me worked like a charm. My mind is completely on the two people in this room.

When her tank top is pulled up to her chest, and the tits we've become obsessed with are free, our eyes drop to them. We both lean forward as our hands move slowly down her sides to her perky little ass. We each take one nipple into our mouth and suck.

Hard.

"Oh!" Mariah jerks into us. Her fingers dig into my shoulder, and I can't help but desperately want them gripping my cock. I want to watch her unravel as we get her off while she strokes us both until we explode.

I nip her nipple, making her moan and jerk into us again. I grab her wrist and move it down my chest until she's right above where I want her to be. I glance over and notice her other hand has followed my motions and is hovering just over all of Matt's ten-inch length. I don't bring her any further than that because she needs to be willing to do what I want her to. I won't force it.

I grip her ass and rub as we both suck her nipples. I flick my tongue over it, making it pebble even more. Mariah tastes like the sweetest treat I've ever had the pleasure of devouring. I don't know how skin can taste like a vanilla latte, but holy shit, it's fucking delectable. I'll never get enough of her.

"Good Christ, you taste so fucking good, baby girl," Matt rumbles. He lightly swats her ass and grips it, making me groan.

"Oh God…," she moans. With shaky hands, she grips our cocks and starts stroking, rotating her wrist.

"Oh fuck, baby," I moan against her.

Matt groans again and lets out an audible gasp. "Fuck, that feels better than in my dreams."

Mariah giggles. "You dream about me…?"

"Every night, beautiful," Matt says.

She strokes faster, and I can't fight anymore. Still gripping her ass, I let my other hand trail up her thigh. I tentatively run my thumb over her pussy. A shiver rolls through my whole body when she spreads her legs even more. I kiss up her chest to her neck. My thumb meets Matt's as he explores her like I am. She's so fucking wet.

Matt kisses up her collarbone to the other side of her neck. She shivers and lets out a sexy, breathy moan. She keeps stroking us, moving her hand all the way up and all the way down our shafts. At the same time, Matt and I slide our middle finger deep inside her pussy, bringing out another moan from her. Her eyes flutter closed, and she shudders around us. She squeezes our dicks a little tighter as she moves her hips in time to our thrusts.

"Mmm…" She lets her head fall back, giving us more access to her neck and throat. Her long, beautiful, chestnut hair brushes over our hands that are firmly gripping her ass. Her pussy clenches and pulses around us, making my dick harder. Precome seeps from my tip.

I start thrusting into her hand as I nibble and suck on her neck. Matt licks and nips at her throat. We both start thrusting faster. Like the good girl she is, she keeps up with our pace and strokes us just as fast as we're thrusting. We both crook our fingers against her G-spot and set our thumbs against her clit. We flick it back and forth, taking turns rubbing it. It causes her thighs to start trembling. Her pussy clenches even tighter around us.

My dick thickens even more. "Fuck, baby, I'm gonna come."

"Holy shit, me too," Matt moans.

Mariah's whole body trembles as she moans. "I'm… oh… my… M-Matt… DJ…" She thrusts over us erratically as she fucks our fingers.

"Come for us, sweet girl," I command.

"Fuck, I need to feel you come, baby," Matt rumbles as we keep thrusting hard, deep, and fast.

Mariah throws her head back. Her pussy spasms around our fingers as she jerks over us and soaks our fingers and thighs. "Oh! Matt! DJ!" she cries out. She keeps jerking our cocks until we both start coming all over her hand and our stomachs.

"Fuck! Mariah!" Matt moans as he thrusts his dick into her hand.

"Christ, Mariah!" I rumble against her neck as I kiss it. She keeps stroking slowly, helping us come down, but making a mess of herself and us.

After a few moments, she stops stroking us as we slowly pull out of her. She looks at us with a shy blush as we suck her off our finger but makes our eyebrows shoot clear to the ceiling when she starts licking our come off her hands.

"Fuck, baby," Matt says with a grin. "You trying to make us come again?"

Mariah giggles as she sits on our thighs with that shy smile I find so fucking sexy. "No… But I've never wanted to taste come before. Everything is so different with you both. It comes so naturally. Like all of this was just meant to be. I don't completely understand it. I've never really been in this situation before. With my other relationships…" She trails off and shrugs. "I guess with the first one, I just wasn't ready. I didn't have the desire. And then with the one I married, I did it because I thought I was supposed to. I got married because I was pushed into it. I feel really bad because I was never really attracted to him. Maybe that's why he -"

"Stop," I rumble warningly, knowing exactly where she's about to go. "You may have been attracted to him in the beginning, but things change, baby. And that's okay. No one would ever blame you for becoming less and less attracted to a man who said you're pussy smells or you're fat."

"And as for the other guy, honey," Matt begins. "I get the friends with benefits thing, but when you start to feel that all he wants from you is sex, there's nothing wrong with becoming disenchanted with the entire thing. You deserve so much better than what you had, beautiful girl. And we weren't kidding when we told you we're going to show you your worth. Because your worth is invaluable, Mariah."

She bites her lip with a soft smile. We both grin and guide her up. We lead her to the bathroom to clean up. After we both get a taste of the sweetest pussy we've ever had the pleasure of eating, we snuggle her into us both on the couch all prepared for a lazy Saturday.

As if to ruin my day, though, my phone vibrates on the table in front of me. I sigh and answer it when I see who it is. "I'm hoping you're about to tell me you found him."

"SWAT has gone through every apartment we could. We've searched the entire building. We don't know how they got out or if someone is hiding him, but he's gone."

"If you searched the apartments and whole building and no one saw him leave, how the fuck is he gone?"

Mariah whimpers and sniffles, sinking deeper into us. We both hug her tighter as she mumbles something I can't quite make out into my chest.

"Some people didn't answer the doors, Cap. We don't know if they aren't home or just wouldn't answer. We can't exactly go busting in doors. There is one thing, though."

"Tell me," I growl.

"There's a possibility he got on the roof. We're not sure how yet, but I'm pulling building surveillance. Building security said a silent alarm sounded on the Southeast corner of the building indicating that the roof access had been breached. They don't know how because you need a keycard and a code to get through. We checked the roof. There's no indication anyone is up there, but we did see what we think are footprints near the edge. We can't tell because it looks more like feet were dragging or some shit, but we have partials. We're trying to lift them. We're also printing the access door."

"You think they jumped buildings?" I wouldn't think that's possible, considering there's several feet between the buildings, but maybe it's more feasible than I can envision.

"I do. We weren't focused on other buildings, but there's evidence pointing to a jump."

I sigh. "Thank you, Tanner. Keep me updated." I hang up and kiss Mariah's head. She's trembling and gripping the band of my sweatpants with all her strength.

Matt looks at me as he pulls Mariah's favorite fleece blanket over us all. "What did he say?"

"That Camden slipped away once again." I quickly text Tanner to get a warrant for Camden. He's armed and dangerous and tried to break into Mariah's apartment. Mariah sniffles once more and snuggles closer to both of us as we wrap around her. "We'll find him, baby. And you're not going to be alone."

"We're not leaving your side, pretty girl," Matt assures her.

That's the damn truth. I don't even need to tell him that we've just put ourselves on bodyguard duty. As a thought strikes me, though, I find myself shooting off another text. I don't know what Camden will do. We need someone on Lyric and Kieran. Will he go to the hospital to start trouble? I have no idea, but I'm not risking it. Not when my family is involved.

I feel a lot lighter, despite the dark cloud that is Camden the Asshole looming over us. No matter what the future holds, we'll fight it together.

Trusting my partners to help me protect my family, I allow myself to slightly relax as we tell Mariah what happened. It's all important, but in this moment, the only thing I care about is showing Mariah how deeply we're falling in love with her.

All that matters is us.

Chapter Nine

☆ Matt ☆

(Four Days Later)

I nibble Mariah's neck as I pin her against the kitchen counter and tickle her. She laughs and wiggles, trying to get away. DJ is in Mariah's living room grinning from ear to ear as he puts the game on. Tampa is playing San Francisco and Mariah just informed us that she's rooting for the 49ers because their quarterback is cuter. We all know she's kidding, but I'll take any excuse I can to touch her.

"Matt! Stop!" Mariah squeals as she attempts to push me away. Not happening. I'm over a foot taller than she is and weigh twice as much as she does.

"Nope. Not until you take back such a rude comment and apologize like a good girl." I press against her a little more, relishing in the feel of her body against mine. Everytime she pushes against me, it makes my dick harder.

She squeals and almost drops to her knees as she laughs. "Okay! Okay! Stop!" She laughs harder.

I stop and lock my arms around her. I kiss the tip of her nose with a grin. "Say it."

She bites her lip with a teasing smile. "My cookies are gonna burn. And then DJ is gonna be sad." She gives me an adorable frown and looks at the oven as if she's mourning the loss of the cookies I know aren't done yet.

"Then you should probably say it so we don't make DJ sad."

She looks up at me, a smirk in her pretty blue eyes. "It's so we don't make DJ sad."

DJ barks out a laugh as I crack up. "You asked for that one!" DJ laughs harder.

Mariah ducks out of my arms giggling and grabs a hot pad as she opens the oven. She takes out the steaming cookies, and I almost forget the entire purpose of the banter and tickling. They smell better than any cookie I've ever eaten. And I've eaten many in my forty-one years.

"Holy shit, those smell fucking amazing." I sniff the air. "Seriously, DJ, she might have your sugar cookies beat." I glance over at him just as his mouth drops.

"Not possible. Take it back, or I'll have you over my knee before you can say sugar cookie."

Mariah giggles again as I grin. "I don't know. I've been told to put them in baking contests. They're soft, melt in your mouth, gooey deliciousness." She puts another tray of cookies in the oven and closes the oven door before turning to me with another adorable smirk and a devilish glint in her pretty blue eyes. "Perfect for when Tampa kicks the shit out of the 49ers."

I laugh. "That's better!" I make a move to steal one of the cookies that she's moving to a cooling rack.

"Don't you dare, Chance!" Mariah says with wide eyes as she guards the cookies. "Make yourself useful and grab the meat and cheese dip or out of my kitchen!" She pouts so prettily that I groan.

"Alright. Fine, fine. I'll be on my best behavior if it means we're getting that seven layer taco dip, too."

"In the fridge just chillin' like..." She tilts her head. "Taco dip." She giggles.

I shake my head as I laugh. I pull out the taco dip as DJ comes in to help. He kisses us both and grips Mariah's ass before he taps it and turns to the meat and cheese dip she's made for nachos. He lifts the lid on the crock pot and stirs it as I start cutting up the peppers Mariah didn't want to. She doesn't do well with peppers and hates the smell of them. She tears up just as she does with onions, which she also hates.

"Alright, baby girl. What's next?" DJ asks, turning the crock pot to warm as he turns.

"Um…" She turns and surveys our spread. We have enough to feed an entire Marine basic unit plus the three of us. "Oh! The wings." She points to the second crock pot filled with unbelievable smelling barbecue wings.

I grin and lift the lid. I stir them so they mix into the sauce even more then take one out to taste test. Mariah giggles and steps next to me. She kisses my arm as I cut into the delectable meat. DJ moves to her and kisses her head as he rests his hand on her ass. I stab some of the chicken with a fork and hold it up to her mouth. She bites into it but says nothing as her eyes widen.

DJ smiles. "Is it good?"

She nods enthusiastically as I give DJ some of it. "So good!" she says as she watches him.

"Holy shit," he rumbles as his smile widens. "That's really good."

I take my bite and moan low. The meat is tender. Juicy. The sauce is sweet with a little heat. "Oh my sweet Jesus." I chew the rest and savor it as I swallow and look down at Mariah. "Not bad for your first time."

She giggles and happily claps her hands as she bounce-walks back to the oven. "I just need the tortilla chips out, and the Fritos scoops out. I'll make the popcorn quick while these cool." She takes out the cookies she had in the oven and turns it off.

"Are you going to let us eat those while they're hot?" DJ asks. "The smell of those things is killing me."

"Wait until you taste them." She beams at us both over her shoulder before turning back around. "You'll get some. Get the other stuff set out and ready. Kick off is soon." She puts the bag of popcorn in the microwave as the cookies she just took out cool.

I raise an eyebrow. "Those look really good. What are they? Looks like they have caramel or something in them."

She nods and hums. "They do. They're white chocolate macadamia nut with caramel drizzled inside them. Well, into the batter.

They're super good. I haven't made them in forever. I thought this would be the perfect opportunity to show off my limited baking skills and make you both fall in love with me."

DJ and I both laugh. "Hate to break it to you, pretty girl. We're already in love with you." DJ leans down and kisses her as he reaches behind her and sneakily steals a sugar cookie. When he pulls back, he breaks the cookie in half high enough above her head that she can't reach it.

Her mouth drops as he hands the other half to me. "Oh my God. Cheater! Manipulator! Thief!" she teases as she giggles. We both shove the cookie in our mouths and give her simultaneous winks.

"Damn," I moan. "They're still warm. Fucking delicious. I was right. They rival yours, Cap. You got yourself some competition."

DJ laughs while Mariah puts the popcorn in a bowl and sprinkles it with M&Ms. "There is no competition. She beats my recipe hands down. These are really good."

We spend the next few minutes helping Mariah set up the food on the coffee table in her living room. We settle into each other with our plates just as Kickoff starts, and we all fall into a peaceful and easy, teasing banter as the game is played.

★★★

After the game has long ended and we've cleaned up the snacks, Mariah collapses in my lap. I wrap my arms around her and kiss her neck. DJ sits with a yawn next to me. He rests a hand on her bare thigh. We're both big fans of her walking around wearing just a pair of panties and one of our t-shirts, hoodies, or in this case, one of our jerseys.

"Why did that game seem so long?" Mariah asks.

"I don't know, but it was fun watching Tampa hand the 49ers their asses on a nicely wrapped silver platter," I say with a grin as I kiss her neck again. I love when she shivers and hums for me.

DJ sighs as he puts down his phone. "I wish they'd find that fucker already. No sign of him. I can't fucking believe it," he mumbles.

Mariah leans over and nuzzles him. "It's scary, but we have to trust that they will, and be on guard." She kisses his jaw. "They'll find him. They have to."

We both know she's pretending to be stronger than she actually is. Especially when she shifts so she's snuggled into both of us. DJ cups her chin and kisses her deeply. I run my hand up and down her back as she moans and whimpers into his kiss.

He pulls away slowly as he hugs her. "The good news is that Lyric is showing signs of waking up. She's not there yet, but they don't think she'll take long."

Mariah smiles. "That's not good news. It's incredible news."

"It really is," I say, breathing a sigh of relief. "I'm happy to hear she's coming around." I rub Mariah's hip.

She's positioned herself so she's sitting sideways between my legs with her hip against my dick. She's leaning over and resting her head on DJ's chest and absently tracing the outline of his length, which is showing off proudly in his gray joggers. I never really understood the entire man in gray sweatpants thing until I saw DJ in them. He's a big guy with a long, thick cock to match the rest of him. I became a fan of gray sweatpants that day and haven't looked back since.

"What are you trying to do to me, beautiful?" DJ rumbles as he watches her small fingers.

She freezes and looks up at him shyly. "Sorry. I wasn't paying much attention. I got lost in thought."

If it were any other woman, I'd believe she's lying, but not Mariah. She's so purely innocent when it comes to sex and flirting that I know damn well she's telling the truth when she says she didn't realize what she was doing.

We've had sex with Mariah a couple of times over the last few days. She won't let either of us near her ass, but she loves sucking one of our cocks while the other is pounding her sweet little pussy. While we both love the time we're getting with her both individually and together, the one thing we're incredibly happy about is how comfortable she is with us. How much she has let herself go with us and opened up to us. How trusting she is with us.

It's a trust we'll never break.

"You're driving me crazy, baby," DJ rumbles as he pulls her into his lap.

I grin at her squeak as she scrambles for purchase, bracing herself on DJ's shoulders with wide eyes. We may have been with her together in various ways, but there's one thing we haven't done that we've been dying to.

I shift and straddle DJ behind Mariah. I grip the hem of my Bucs jersey that she confiscated today and tug it off. "I really want to feel your tight little pussy stretched around us both." I toss the jersey and start undoing the clasps of her bra as she gives us a sexy, quiet moan. I know my girl. She's loving the idea of that.

"How attached are you to these panties?" DJ rumbles against her lips just before he takes them in a hard, all-consuming kiss that makes her whimper submissively.

He hooks his thumb in the waistband of the barely there lace panties. I toss the bra once it's off and let my hands slide down her sides. I hook my thumbs in her panties as he pulls away slowly from the kiss.

"N-Not very...," she whispers shyly. Without another word, DJ and I tear the panties. "Oh my God!" She's already trembling for us, but when she looks over her shoulder at me with wide eyes, I can see the heat in them.

DJ leans forward and starts teasing her nipples with his tongue as he strokes his cock. He slowly slides himself inside her with a low groan. She moans and closes her eyes, arching into him. I lean forward and kiss her neck. I let my hands make their way up her body to her luscious mounds. While DJ continues lavishing her nipples, I rub her tits, gently squeezing them.

I nip her neck. "Think you can take both of us?" I rumble, sending shivers down her spine.

"U-um..." She looks at us both, hesitation and confusion written all over her.

DJ thrusts into her slowly, helping her to relax. "He means both of us in your pussy at the same time. We respect you, baby. Your ass is off limits."

I rub my hands slowly up and down her body, helping her to relax even more. I know how tight she is. Her taking us both would feel fucking incredible to us, but we'd never want to rip her apart for our own pleasure.

"I… want to… try…" She looks at us both shyly as she relaxes and melts into us more and more.

"You have no idea how happy I am to hear you say that," I whisper in her ear.

DJ continues slowly thrusting, coating them both in her wetness, and making it easier for me when she's ready for me to slide into her. I brace myself on the couch and slide my dick between her thighs to coat myself in her wetness. Nibbling her neck, I use my dick to tease them both, driving them even crazier as they both moan.

DJ rumbles low as he watches his dick slowly pumping into her pussy and mine rubbing against her and him. She starts moving against him, making herself wetter for us both. She reaches behind her and grips my thigh, her other hand still using DJ for support.

"Fuck…, Matt. I need to feel you both," DJ groans as he lets his head fall back against the back of the couch. One of his hands finds my ass. The other grips her. "She's so wet." He meets my eyes then hers. He leans into her and kisses her so deeply, she gasps.

Feeling that her body is completely relaxed, I use DJ as my guidance that she's ready for me. I grip my dick and angle myself so I'm against her entrance. The feel of my dick resting against DJ's and my tip just touching her pussy, even though I'm not even inside, makes me hard as fucking steel. I breathe out against her neck as I push inside her slowly. DJ pauses his thrusts. Mariah lets out the sexiest whimper moan I've ever heard.

"Oh, Matt… Oh God, Matt…," Mariah gasps. She lets herself fall against DJ's chest. She spreads her legs even wider as she relaxes more and more. It allows me to slide even deeper.

"Holy Christ, sweet girl," I breathe. "Fuck, you're tight."

I feel her softly giggle. "Am I really that tight? Or is it the fact that you and DJ have huge and thick cocks?" Her sassiness and unparalleled humor makes us both crack up. It's a couple of the many things we truly love about her.

"I mean, it could be," I tease. "Or it could be because you're so… fucking… tight…" I push in a little more, grinning against her neck.

"Jesus…," DJ groans. He grips my ass even tighter as his dick twitches and throbs against mine. Her pussy spasms and clenches around us both.

I push in slowly, inch by inch, waiting for her to get used to us and stretch around us before I thrust in any further. When we're finally inside her as far as she can take us, we're all panting. Feeling her pussy squeezing my dick; DJ's dick flexing and jerking against mine is one of the greatest feelings I've ever had the pleasure of experiencing. Neither one of us even has to thrust. I'm already ready to fill her pussy.

"My fuck, pretty girl," I rumble against her shoulder as I meet DJ's eyes.

"Oh...," Mariah rumbles. She buries her head in DJ's neck.

"Doing okay, honey?" I ask her, soothingly rubbing her hips.

She nods and starts slowly moving over us. "Feels... so... oh... so good..."

DJ and I grunt and groan. My eyes roll back in my head when he starts thrusting. I'm no stranger to DJ's dick. This isn't even the first time we've given a vaginal double penetration to a woman. I've felt my cock rubbing against DJ's before.

But something about the way *she* feels wrapped around us while our dick's are rubbing against each other is a feeling in another stratosphere of what I've felt in the past with any other girl. Mariah makes me feel a lot of things I've only ever felt with DJ. She's the completion to our hearts.

Which is probably why the intensity of our love-making feels out of bounds.

We play on her cues so naturally, like we're all one body or something, and thrust faster when she does. We thrust harder when she clenches around us; deeper when she pulses and squeezes our cocks.

"Don't stop," she whispers as she writhes against us. Her nails dig into my thigh as she meets our thrusts. "Don't ever stop!"

DJ starts rolling his hips. I follow his lead and roll mine, in complete harmony with him. Mariah's thighs instantly start to tremble. She soaks our dicks, making each thrust sound like the dirtiest kind of fun I've ever heard. It spurs me on to thrust even harder, giving her all I feel she can take.

"Mariah, baby. Fuck!" DJ slaps her ass and mine at the same time, causing us both to jerk and tumble into him at the pleasurable sensation he sends through us. DJ's dick jerks against mine as it thickens. "Holy shit, Matt." His grip on my ass tightens.

I can't resist anymore. I lean in and kiss him long and deeply as we both fuck Mariah's tight pussy. I suck on his tongue and let him fuck my mouth with his. As soon as I pull back, my lips are on Mariah's. DJ might get to dominate our kiss, but I dominate mine and Mariah's. As DJ had with me seconds ago, I begin a sexy tango with her tongue as we both thrust into her.

I feel the very moment she loses control. Her entire body jerks. Her pussy clamps hard around us both. Her eyes widen as I kiss her. DJ takes turns sucking on both of our necks. I don't realize right away that he's moved his hand from her ass as we claim her pussy in the most intimate of ways to her clit. He's rubbing it in time to our rhythm.

"Fuck, baby. Come. Come for us. Come all over our cocks, beautiful," DJ moans.

I swallow her screams as I kiss her. She stiffens enough to make my spine tingle. Before I know it, DJ grips my ass, forcing me to hold still deep inside her pussy. The tingle turns into a full jolt that shoots down my spine. I pull back just as her pussy begins to spasm and pulse around us while she comes.

"DJ! Matt! Oh my fuck! Yes!" Mariah's hips jerk into ours as she comes hard for us.

Her pussy tightening and DJ's thick dick against mine is all I need to lose my own control. "Fuck! Holy fuck, Mariah! DJ!" I groan. As soon as I feel DJ's come shooting into her, I let my own load fly.

"Oh, Christ, Mariah! Matt!"

We both jerk against her as we all ride our high. After several moments of quiet moans and soft panting, DJ and I let ourselves slip out of her pussy. I collapse on the couch next to them, rubbing Mariah's thigh. DJ holds her tightly, rubbing her back soothingly as our come drips down her thigh.

I've never felt so at peace.

But the serenity doesn't last long. Just as we're all fully relaxed and snuggled with each other, a loud bang on the door makes us all jump. Mariah squeaks. DJ holds her tighter as I position my body in front of them both.

"Mariah! I know you're in there, bitch!" Camden screams as he bangs on the door. "Open the fucking door!"

Mariah screams, but hides it behind her hand as she jumps off DJ with wide eyes. She looks at both of us. I hate seeing the fear and terror there.

DJ and I both launch off the couch. We each take one of her hands and push her in front of us towards the bedroom.

"Go!" DJ hisses. He doesn't need to make the command twice. Mariah sprints to her bedroom. We both follow at a dead run behind her.

As soon as we get there, a gunshot rings through the air. This time, Mariah doesn't hide the scream as she falls to the floor covering her ears. The scream is high-pitched. Animalistic. I don't even think she realizes she's screaming.

DJ leaps over her, diving for our guns as I use the wall for cover and turn around. I peer behind the wall, but quickly move back behind it, keeping the door mostly closed, as another shot rings out.

"Too fucking late, little bitch!" Camden screams. "You're fucking dead now!"

"Matt!" DJ hisses as he hands me my gun. He crouches down and positions himself between Mariah and me, his gun in his hand and leveled at the door, backing me up.

I peer around the wall again when I hear something crash. My eyes widen when I see Camden standing in the living room. He has a bottle in his hand with a cloth hanging out of it. He's holding a lighter in the other hand. There's a gun at his hip stuck in the waistband of his jeans.

"Oh, shit," I whisper when I realize what the fuck it is. Continuing to use the wall for cover, I take aim, intending to shoot the fucker between the eyes.

But I don't get the chance.

Before I can shoot, Camden's eyes meet mine. They're cold. Calculating. And the smirk he gives me is the most evil I've ever seen. He throws the freshly lit concoction right at me as he laughs like a madman. I have no choice but to close the door and lock it, praying to whatever God exists that the explosion doesn't take out the door. It's our only protection from the flames now.

I look back at DJ trying to keep the fear in my eyes at bay as I take a deep, calming breath. It doesn't fucking work. Not even a little. I'm panicking. Not because the apartment outside these walls is on fire. Not because we're trapped inside this room.

It's because I know *exactly* what's about to happen to Mariah.

I can do all I can to keep the flames out.

I would shoot if Camden decides to be brave and come after us through the flames he set in the hall.

I wouldn't think twice about any measure of protection I need to take to keep us all safe.

What terrifies me is this will send Mariah straight into a PTSD induced panic attack.

One she'll never wake up from.

Chapter Ten

☆ Mariah ☆

As soon as we reach the bedroom, either DJ or Matt propels me through the door. Another loud bang that sounds way too much like a gunshot rings out. I fall to the ground screaming as I cover my ears. I curl into myself and contort my body as small as I can.

Tears stream down my face.

I try to stop screaming, but I can't. I rock myself back and forth. I keep my head down and ears covered.

He's shooting! Why is he shooting? I scream the words, but I know they're only in my head. I can't actually get them to formulate enough to come out of my mouth.

My demon is chuckling. I can hear him. He says nothing, but he's at the forefront of my mind. It's like he's watching everything unfold, and I'm trapped somewhere within myself.

As crazy as it sounds, I'm fine with that. He can take complete control for all I care. As long as I'm away from it all and completely detached from it.

I know something bad is happening around me. The gunshots have stopped. Matt or DJ just slammed the door shut. There's chaos. Both of them are saying something. I feel someone grab me around the waist and move me, but I can't stop screaming. I try, but fail miserably.

I keep my eyes squeezed close and my ears covered.

My demon literally feels like he's dancing in my head. Like he's doing some kind of ritual. It's fucking crazy to actually feel like this thing inside my mind is real. That he's a separate entity from me. The truth is, if I don't think of him like that, I'll succumb to him. Because then it's like it's me telling myself all of the horrible things he tells me. Who can actually fight oneself? It would be like me fighting with me and killing me. It simply doesn't work that way. I don't care who says it does. If they don't experience it, they don't know.

"Mariah!" DJ barks pinning me against him and a wall.

I jump. My eyes snap to his instantly at his commanding tone. The scream dies in my throat, and I gasp instead. There's a roaring in my mind. Like a train is coming at me and stopping at my station. Like all of me is slamming back into my body.

It makes me jump and stare at him with wonder. How? How did he just pull me back so quickly when I was sunk so deeply in my own mind?

"Baby, you have to focus. I need you present for me if we're getting through this." DJ's voice is low. Dominant. Everything I need.

I nod slowly and focus on him; his sharp, jade eyes. "O-okay," I say shakily. "Okay." My eyes still spill tears.

"Good girl," DJ rumbles. "Buckets. Ice cream buckets. Anything, Mariah. Cups. Do you have anything like that? Jugs you emptied and never threw away. Anything at all."

I blink a few times. The question is bizarre. Buckets? Jugs? Why? I furrow my brows and look around. We're in the bathroom. I don't know how we got in here, but Matt, still completely naked, is filling the bathtub.

I shake my head and look at DJ in complete bewilderment. "I... don't... Why?"

"Please, baby. Tell me you have something. Anything we can use."

I have no clue what's happening, but I trust my boyfriend. "U-um... I... There's ice cream buckets under the sink in here. I had a leak. I never moved them in case it happened again."

"Good girl." DJ takes my hand in his and pulls me with him to the cabinet. He yanks it open and throws the buckets to Matt. Matt dunks them in the water. "Anything else?" DJ looks down at me as he stands, still holding my hand.

I bite my lip, fighting back panic and focusing completely on him. "I… have a vase. It's a large one. It's on the dresser in the bedroom." I start to lead him out of the bathroom, but he tugs me back.

"No, baby. You need to stay here."

The look in his eyes makes my heart beat faster. I pause and obey. DJ takes the freshly filled buckets from Matt and quickly exits the bathroom. I put my hand on the counter and rub my chest with my other one as I take a deep breath. I'm starting to feel lightheaded. I still haven't totally come back to myself.

I look up at Matt when he wraps his arms around me. "Where's Camden?" I whisper against his chest.

"Not here anymore, baby. He took off. He's not the threat anymore, but he gave us a huge fucking new one." Matt breathes deeply as he kisses my neck. I know he's using my scent to steady himself because it's the exact same thing I do with him.

I hear DJ slamming drawers in the bedroom and cursing, though he's still speaking in a completely normal voice. I try to look at him, but Matt doesn't allow me to turn my head. His fingers are tangled in my hair, and he's holding me firmly as he sways with me.

DJ hurriedly comes back in without the buckets. He has an armful of clothing and several things he can put water in. The large vase I bought at a flea market, another smaller one, and a couple of cups that we keep in the bedroom for if we wake in the middle of the night and need something to drink.

"Get dressed. Hurry up," DJ commands. He sets everything on the counter, grabbing all of the things he can put water in. He puts them into the bathtub, then turns and starts getting dressed himself.

I still don't have a fucking clue what's going on, but the three of us dress in record time. After Matt and DJ finish, they both strap their guns to their waist. Why that sight comforts me so much is something so many just don't get. But to me, those guns means not only can these two men protect me, but they can also protect themselves and each other.

I watch as Matt pops his head out the door. DJ opens the linen closet and pulls out three of my spare, King-sized pillowcases. I furrow my brows at him but bite my lip. Whatever is happening, I trust them above all else. I know they love me and care about me, but more than that, I know they'll do all they can to make sure all of us are safe.

DJ dips the pillowcases into the water, soaking them. Matt takes as many of the filled containers as he can carry and quickly moves to the bedroom. DJ rings the excess water out of the pillowcases. After folding them in half the long way, he moves to me.

"This goes around your nose and mouth. Under no circumstances do you take this off. Understand?"

My eyes widen. I whimper as what's happening suddenly slams into me. "He started a fire…," I whisper. "That's why you need the water."

"Mariah, baby, please. Do as I say. Turn around." DJ's voice is soft, but it still holds the dominance I need to cut through everything I'm thinking and feeling.

I nod and close my eyes as I swallow and turn around. "Yes, sir," I whisper.

DJ makes quick work of tying it behind my head. It's tight, but I know it's so it won't fall off. "Breathe through your nose. I need you to be a good girl. Stay strong. And no matter what happens, you need to know that Matt and I will always keep you safe. Panic will cause you to breathe faster, but we can't allow that. We need you to keep breathing through your nose, which will also help with that pulse rate. Understand?"

I open my eyes and meet his in the mirror. "Yes, sir."

"Good girl." He and Matt put theirs on.

"Tell me one of you has your phone in here," Matt says as he searches through all of the cabinets, looking for something only he seems to know.

"Mariah's is on the nightstand. It was charging."

"Thank fuck," Matt growls. DJ runs to the bedroom for my phone. I glance into the room after him. I can see some smoke, but it doesn't seem to be too terrible. "Baby, anything else in here? Jugs? Cups? Anything at all."

I shake my head and wipe my eyes. "I'm sorry."

"Don't, baby. This isn't your fault."

It is. This is all on you, my demon hisses.

Matt wraps his arms around me and whispers in my ear. "It's not your fault, baby. This is fucking Camden and his insanity. Not you."

And just like that, the demon is gone. Banished to the depths of my mind where he goes back to giddily dancing all over the chaos.

He's still somehow making me feel like I'm detached from this situation, though. I may not like his voice telling me things, like what a fuck up I am, or how this is all my fault, but I'll happily let him take control of me if it means I don't have to deal with what's happening on some level. At least enough so I can stay calm enough to help them like they need me to.

To be strong.

Their good girl.

I know I can be.

"Her bedroom," DJ says into my phone. Matt and I both look at him. "How the fuck am I supposed to know that? I locked us in her bedroom. The entire front part of the apartment and hallway is probably fully fucking engulfed. Tanner, you need to get us out of here, man."

The words are enough to make my heart race even faster. I cling to Matt and gasp out a sob, but I make myself keep breathing through my nose. Just like DJ said.

I'm their good girl.

We both keep watching DJ. He pinches the bridge of his nose. "Tell them to mobilize faster. Get them a block. Fuck, I don't care. We don't have time." DJ's eyes meet mine, and I pull as much strength from that one encouraging look as I can. "Do it, Sergeant Ryan. Number one priority for you. Let the fucking Captain command everything else." He drops the phone into his back pocket, his eyes never leaving mine. "I can't leave you in here, sweet girl. And I need Matt out there. You're not going to like what you see, but you have to stay strong, baby."

I nod. "I will," I say resolutely. I *will* be their good girl.

Matt kisses my head and leads me to the bedroom. As soon as we cross the threshold from the bathroom to the bedroom, I can feel the heat difference. It's staggering. I squeeze Matt's hand tighter and whimper. I expect to see flames all around the room, but I don't. It's just starting to fill with smoke.

A lot of it.

I make the mistake of glancing towards the door. Through the cracks, I can see that it's glowing red-orange. I squeeze Matt's hand tighter. "Oh my God."

Matt pulls me closer to his body as he and DJ lead me towards the balcony door. I can hear that roaring again. Only it's not in my head this time. The heat from the fire out there is making it hotter in here. I'm positive the walls are scorching to the touch, but I don't go near them. I don't have to. I can see the waves from the heat in the room. It feels way more than a hundred degrees.

I glance at the clock on the wall. It's one of those Timex clocks that sets itself in ways I'll never understand. Something about Atomic time. It tells me the date. It even tells me the room temperature.

Or it would… if it wasn't melting off the wall.

How hot does it have to be for a clock to begin melting off a wall? I ask myself, morbidly fascinated as I allow Matt to lead me.

Hot, my demon answers. *So, fucking hot. Doesn't it feel great in here? Fuck, it's like I'm right at home. You know you're going to die. But I'll live on and on and on. Right here. Just like this. While the flames lick your body and you scream in agony and writhe in pain, I'll be thriving.*

Shut-up.

"I want you right here," DJ says as Matt pulls me in front of him, shielding me from the stupid clock.

I blink up at him, then glance out the door. "Why not outside?" I ask quietly. *Anywhere but here.*

Matt and DJ exchange a look. Matt clears his throat and wraps his arms around me. "Because as soon as we open that door, we're introducing a whole lot of oxygen into a situation where there isn't a lot. The fire is sucking it all up. It's getting hotter and hotter because it has a lot of fuel to use. The carpet. Furniture. That's why the door is glowing; why it feels so hot in here. And why that clock is starting to melt off the wall. That wall itself isn't going to last much longer. We're probably going to have a flashover soon. And when that happens, I pray to anyone listening that the fire department is here. Because we'll need to get out. Fast."

"When we open this door, we're risking a backdraft. We're allowing cool air to enter a very volatile, superheated situation."

I swallow.

Hard.

But I take a deep breath through my nose and nod. It's all I can do.

"I want you on the ground. As low as you can get," Matt says.

DJ glances over Matt's shoulder then rushes to push me to the ground. "On your stomach so you can quickly get up and crawl when you need to. The fire department is on the way." He hands me my phone. "Dial the last number in there. It's Sergeant Ryan. Tell him to talk to you. You need him to keep you calm."

I nod and do as I'm told. I lay flat on my stomach and dial the last number in my phone to have been called. I put it on speaker so I don't need to hold it. I might need my hands. DJ and Matt move towards the door. Flames have started to come through the bottom of it. I sniffle and force myself to look away as they start using the water to douse the flames and keep them from coming in here. I'm not sure it will do much good.

"Ryan," a deep voice barks.

"S-Sergeant Ryan?" I clear my throat. Even with the pillowcase around my nose and mouth, my throat feels scratchy. My eyes burn. I sniffle.

"Mariah? What's going on?"

"D-DJ s-said to call. Keep me calm. T-talk to me."

"Okay. Okay, sweetheart. How about you tell me what's happening? And I'll tell you what I'm doing to help."

I nod, then realize he can't see me. "It's hot."

"Are you still in your bedroom?"

"Yes, sir." I cough. "Lots of smoke now. The clock on the wall is m-melting. They're th-throwing water at the f-flames sneaking under the door."

"We're coming, Mariah. I promise you, we're coming. We caught Camden. We got a call from one of the residents that they saw him on the premises. We had lots of people watching out for him. The woman called right away. We were already there when he started the fire, honey. The fire department is here. They're setting up."

I nod and squeeze my eyes closed, then remember again that he can't see me. "Okay." I glance at DJ and Matt.

The roaring is so loud now. I can't even hear myself think, but I hear something explode outside the walls. The floor shakes. More smoke billows into the room, and I scream when I see more flames licking the door and crawling across the walls.

"Talk to me, Mariah!" Sergeant Ryan's voice cuts through the panic that's already risen to a level I'm not certain how I'm surviving.

"Flames!" I shriek. "Matt and DJ are throwing as much water as they can, but there's so much smoke!" I start sobbing. "I can't even see them!" I start to get up, to search for them, but then remember DJ's words.

I need you to be a good girl. Stay strong. And no matter what happens, you need to know that Matt and I will always keep you safe.

I need to be their good girl.

"We're almost there, Mariah! We need to be fast! Can DJ and Matt hear me?" Sergeant Ryan asks.

"We can hear you!" Matt yells.

"Get us fucking help, Sergeant! Move it!" DJ yells right after.

"Thank God," I whisper. I can't see them. The smoke is too thick. But thank God I can hear their voices.

"You all need to listen to me!" Sergeant Ryan yells. "Fire is set up right outside Mariah's apartment! Everyone in the building has been evacuated! I need to know what everything looks like! I have the Fire Captain with me!"

"Dense smoke!" DJ yells. "It's billowing from under the door! Flames, but not many! Just around the door! We're combating them, but smoke is getting worse! A lot thicker! It's fucking hot! The clock on the wall the fire is raging on the other side of is nothing more than plastic dripping down the fucking wall!"

"We don't have any time or the ability to vent!" another voice that I assume is the Fire Captain barks. "We only have one shot at this! All three of you need to get out the balcony door at the same time! Run and jump! Bend your legs! Cover your head! Turn yourself in the air so you'll land on your side! It's the safest way to fall without safety equipment!"

Another explosion.

I scream and stare in horror at the place where the door was. It glows even more orange, and flames shoot into the room.

"DJ! Matt!" I cough and scream their names again when they don't answer. "DJ! Matt!" The smoke is black. The room is so dark, I can't see anything, and I'm getting lightheaded.

"Mariah!" Sergeant Ryan yells.

I can't even see the phone anymore. I'm disoriented. Sweating. My clothes are sticking to me. "DJ! Matt!" I scream and cry.

"Mariah! Tell me what happened!" Sergeant Ryan yells.

"Explosion!" I cry. "I can't hear them!"

I hear a crack and jerk my head towards the balcony door. Bright, white light shines through it, like a beacon, but the window is cracked.

"Oh fuck," Sergeant Ryan breathes. "Mariah, the door. Is the glass cracked? We can't tell from down here, but it looks like it is."

"Y-yes."

"Fuck, Mariah. You guys have to get out! Scream for them again!"

But I can't.

"Mariah!"

The light dims slowly as my world starts to turn as black as the room.

"Mariah!"

My lungs burn like they're on fire. I can't scream anymore. I can hardly see.

"Mariah! Fuck! Answer me, honey! Scream for them again!"

I can't even breathe...

Chapter Eleven

☆ DJ ☆

"Fuck," Matt rumbles as he runs back out of the bathroom with refilled buckets.

"I know," I growl as I run into the bathroom to refill mine.

We've been taking turns running in and out of the bathroom to refill the containers we were blessed by all the fucking powers in the world to find. I run back out as the Fire Captain barks out falling orders. It's all shit we've already been trained on with our SWAT training, but I hope to hell that Mariah is listening closely.

My arms burn. I'm out of breath. My chest is burning from the smoke and the exertion. My arms hurt just as bad from the constant motion of filling the shit with water and throwing it at the damn door.

When I get my hands on Camden, I'll fucking kill him. Who the hell does this? Matt told me what happened as soon as we got Mariah on the ground. Motherfucker threw Molotov cocktails all around the damn apartment. Not only is he putting our lives in jeopardy, but he's putting all of the residents who live here in danger.

I'm bringing attempted murder charges on him. Two hundred fucking counts of it. One for every single person in this building and two more Lyric and Kieran. I don't give a shit if the District Attorney laughs my ass out of his office. I'm charging him for every single life he's fucked over.

After the thousandth time of filling the buckets, I'm fucking done. Matt and I are slowing down, losing more and more energy the longer we're forced to wait for the Fire Department to get set up and give us the go. There has already been one explosion in the other room. I'm positive it was a flashover. With how fucking hot it is in here, I know damn well it's a lot hotter out there.

Matt and I are both coughing and starting to stumble. When I see him coming into the bathroom as I'm leaving it once more, I make a decision that I really didn't want to. But we can't fucking wait anymore. We need to get to the balcony door with Mariah and get the fuck out of here.

"No more," I say, grabbing his arm. "We're done. Time to get out. We're too close to passing out."

"They haven't given us the go ahead. We can't just run and take a flying leap, hoping they're ready. And we need to keep the flames as much at bay as we can." His voice is just as raspy as mine. We both cough weakly.

I shake my head. My arms are shaking. "We need to get out." I drop my hand to his and link our fingers tightly. I pull him in the direction of the patio, but I'm going completely off instinct because I'm disoriented and can't see a fucking thing.

Just as we're nearing the bedroom door, another explosion outside the walls shakes the ground. Matt and I are thrown backwards as the door careens off its hinges and shatters into a bunch of flaming pieces.

Flames shoot into the room.

It all seems to go in slow motion.

I hear Mariah scream, but it sounds deep and far away.

I see the flames licking up the walls, but it looks like they've been put on pause.

I hit a wall behind me so hard, I'm certain my lungs have exited my chest cavity and come out my mouth. Matt grunts, and I pray like fuck that he didn't hit his head on anything.

Somehow, we're still tightly gripping each other's hands. Something else to thank the powers that be for.

But not now. Right now, we need to get the fuck out.

"DJ! Matt!" Mariah shrieks. Her voice is starting to crack. I hope she hasn't inhaled as much smoke as us.

"Here, Mariah!" I croak, but I can barely hear myself. No way in hell she can.

"Oh, fuck…" Matt groans. He tugs on my hand as he moves. I glance behind me. He was blown into the bathroom. He might have hit his head, but he looks good.

Conscious.

"We need to get out, Matt. Now."

"Yeah."

"DJ! Matt!" Mariah screams again, but it's a lot quieter this time.

"Christ," Matt grunts as he crawls to me. "We need to get out."

I barely hear him. I know he barely hears me, but I grunt in agreement anyway. We both force ourselves to our feet. I use the fire to guide me. The flames are making their way towards the bathroom and the balcony, but I know where I am because of the open door. It may have been a blessing in disguise to have it blown off. It reoriented me.

Matt squeezes my hand as we both run in a crouch towards the balcony. The closer we get, the more light we see. It looks like the fire department has a spotlight on the door. I'm thankful because it gives us the light we need to make it the rest of the way.

"Mariah! Fuck! What's happening!" Tanner screams over the phone.

I nearly choke out a sob when I see her lying unmoving by the door. "Fuck, Ryan, get us out of here!" I rasp.

"Jesus Christ, Cap, thank God," he says. It actually sounds like he's been crying. "Get out of there! The window is cracking! You're going to have a backdraft as soon as the fucking door opens, but you need to get out! You have to jump!"

I glance out the window as Matt wastes no time picking Mariah up in his arms. The balcony is made of concrete. We can easily get up on the barrier and jump. The problem is that one of us will need to jump with Mariah. Which means we need to move even more quickly since we can't all jump up there together. Matt will need to hand her to me and then get up on the ledge himself. We'll have less than ten seconds before the backdraft happens.

I nod to myself. "Hand her to me as soon as I get up on the ledge. Get up there fast. We'll have less than ten seconds to jump."

"Got it," Matt rumbles.

"You better be ready for us, Ryan," I grunt.

"We're ready, Cap. Just fucking jump. We have a lot of guys down here ready to move the thing if necessary. We have two of them, so when you jump, try to do it apart from each other. Separate sides of the balcony. We'll catch you."

"You fucking better, or I will personally haunt your ass forever," Matt growls.

"Three… two… one…" As soon as I get to one, I open the door and leap for the ledge.

Matt is on my heels. He hands me Mariah. Even deadweight, she still feels light as a feather to me, but I'm certain it's adrenaline because I'm fucking sore. Tired. I don't know how the hell I'm even still moving.

I meet Matt's eyes. He wastes no time in leaping on the ledge next to me. I glance down. True to his word, Tanner is down there with the Fire Captain looking up at us. There are a lot of firefighters on the ground and two air cushions. They're ready to move if they need to. I've never been so fucking happy to see so many of my brothers who hold the red line.

Taking a breath after making sure Mariah is positioned correctly, with her back to me and feet on the ground, I glance into the bedroom. Flames are licking across the ceiling. The smoke is black but I can see wisps of orange throughout. The roaring sounds like a damn tornado. I take one more glance at Matt and jump at the same time he does. I tuck Mariah into my body so I can protect her on the landing as best as I can. It doesn't matter that we're jumping from about forty feet into a giant air cushion. It still fucking hurts if the land is wrong. Injuries can still happen.

But I'll take a busted arm or cracked rib over dying in an explosion any fucking day of the week.

And an explosion is exactly what happens.

I feel the heat on my back. I tuck myself over Mariah even more when I see flaming pieces of who the fuck knows raining down on us.

We're getting closer to the air cushion.

Closer.

Closer.

The firefighters are yelling something as they watch us. Some of them move the other cushion. The one not underneath us. My heart is beating out of my chest hoping that we'll be okay. That we'll all be okay. To escape a fire only to die by not hitting the air cushion right. What a cruel world that would be. A cruel fucking twist of dark and evil fate.

I close my eyes just before we hit. The land takes my breath away. For the second time in five minutes, my lungs have relocated and come out my mouth. Organs are shifting to places they don't belong. I think I may have groaned, but my brain still hasn't caught up to the rest of me.

When everything finally stops moving, I dare open my eyes. It's utter chaos. Everyone is talking at once, and I can't understand a single fucking thing anyone is saying. I know I made the landing okay, but I don't know how Mariah did, and I can't see Matt.

A couple of firefighters make it to our sides. One of them tries to pull Mariah from me, but I growl. It must be enough to scare him, because his eyes widen, and he instantly backs off.

"Cap!" Sergeant Ryan yells from above my head.

I tilt my head to look up at him. "Matt." It's the only word I can say.

"Good. He's good. He's up. Walking around. They're checking him out."

"Sir, we need to check you both out," someone says to me. The firefighter who touched Mariah.

"I'm fine," I growl.

"Cap, they need to check her. She passed out just after that second explosion. Come on. Let them check her."

I know Tanner is right, but it doesn't help me to let her go. I'm fucking terrified. I know I'm okay. I know Matt is because I trust my partner wouldn't lie to me. But I don't know if our girl is. I don't know if she'll ever wake up from this. I know exactly the demons she battles when it comes to fire. And I know why. This is something she may never recover from.

Knowing she needs more help than I know how to give her, I hand her off to the professionals, trusting they'll keep our girl breathing. I had my arms locked around her. She wasn't inhaling or exhaling. She needs oxygen. CPR.

And I need to be checked out myself. I groan as I sit up, a firefighter helping me. "Oh, fuck."

"Tell me where it hurts, Captain," he says to me.

"My shoulder. The second explosion blew the door in the bedroom back. The force threw me and Matt backwards. I hit the wall. I thought he might have hit his head on something in the bathroom."

"They're checking him, Sir. Your girl is getting oxygen. They have her breathing, but she hasn't come to. They're working on stabilizing her before they try and wake her. Let's talk about you."

I close my eyes and nod as I swallow. Pain shoots through my head. "Shoulder and neck." I open my eyes. "I think I was okay hitting the wall. Maybe bruised it or something. But when I landed on this, I landed on my shoulder. It feels like something is fucked up. Pain is radiating into my neck."

"Yes, sir. Let's get you off this thing first. Try not to move your arm. Let us slide you down. We'll stabilize you after we get you settled on solid ground."

I just nod and let them do what they need to. I keep my arm as close to my chest as I can and let them move me. They guide me to an ambulance as other firefighters start attacking the fire. I glance up and see that the fire has spread into another apartment. A shuddering sigh escapes because I don't know how we got out alive.

The paramedics try to guide me into an ambulance to work on me, but I just shake my head. "Work on me out here. I need to see them," I croak, nodding towards Matt and Mariah.

The paramedic clears his throat but nods. I'm sure he planned to argue. It would be completely futile. I need to see them. Matt is sitting on the back of an ambulance near me. Mariah is getting loaded onto a stretcher. Time still hasn't quite caught up to itself. I still feel like it's going a lot slower than it should be. Like I'm not even completely inside my own body. An outsider observing the chaos.

When the paramedic is done fussing over Matt, Matt is immediately on his feet. The other paramedics dealing with Mariah quickly move her to a waiting ambulance. Matt stares in openmouthed horror. I can see the tears in his eyes from here.

"We're going with her," I say to the paramedic immobilizing my shoulder.

"I know, sir. Almost done."

"We gotta go, Tim!" someone else yells to the person working on me.

"He's good to go!" the man named Tim says. "Wouldn't matter if I were or weren't. Don't think I'd be keeping you away."

"Not a chance in hell." I give him a weak smile as I stand. I'm not sure if it's good or bad that I can't feel any pain. "Thanks."

"You got it, Cap."

I make my way to the other ambulance and wait for Matt to climb in. I chuckle. "Gonna be a little crowded with all of us."

"Sit, DJ. Please." Matt guides me to the jumper seat and hugs me tight. "Fuck, I love you so much, baby."

I hug him hard with one arm. "I love you, too. So damn much."

His grip loosens after a few moments. He sits on the floor next to me as the ambulance drives off. I take his hand while the paramedic continues monitoring Mariah. Neither one of us speak, but we really don't need to. We know exactly what the other one is thinking.

The first is that our priority right now is making sure we're okay, and that Mariah is okay. The three of us are what's important. Us and our family. Lyric and Kieran. We need to check on Luca and see how he's doing.

The second?

Fucking Camden needs to be annihilated…

Chapter Twelve

★ Matt ★

It's been hours since we escaped the fire in Mariah's apartment. I'm grateful we got out because there was a period of time where I honestly believed we were all going down in a fiery ending.

I'm pissed.

Beyond pissed actually.

How the fuck out of their mind does a person have to be to do what Camden did? To show up at a woman's house with a fucking gun blaming her for him spending a couple of nights in jail for the role he played in literally any incident? How crazy does a person have to be to shoot out locks on a door and start an apartment on fire?

That building has security cameras. Everything he had done was recorded. Both times he showed up with a gun. The banging and pounding on her door. Shooting out the locks. We know when he entered. We know how he got away from us the other times. We even know where he hid when we were canvasing the complex for him. He was probably laughing the entire goddamn time.

The more and more I sit here and think of the events that played out between him and Mariah, the more certain I am that mine and DJ's instincts are right on. Camden was involved in Shannon's murder. Nate's instincts about him were right on.

Since we jumped out of the burning apartment and got to the hospital, it's where we've remained. We were both released long ago, but Mariah is still unconscious. It's mine and DJ's biggest fear playing out in front of our eyes. She's not unconscious because of the smoke inhalation or injury. It's because she panicked so badly and fought it so hard that when the adrenaline was gone, it was it for her.

And now we're here watching two of our loved ones fighting for their lives. Mariah, the other piece of our heart, and Lyric, our little sister. I'm not a man who is afraid of much of anything, but this is terrifying. I'd rather walk through the fire in that apartment again then deal with watching them in this room unmoving.

The hospital bed in this room simply isn't big enough to hold me, DJ, and Mariah. If it were, I'd be wrapped around them both instead of wedged in this nook by the window watching the sun rise of University Hospital. People are hurrying all over the campus. Doctors, nurses, and staff are rushing into the building.

It's a little insane to watch. All of these people scurrying around down there, but up here, it's like time has slowed. The seconds tick by with each beep of machines; each breath we all breathe. It makes me realize that time is fucking fickle. It goes at the pace it wants to.

Which is why we shouldn't waste a fucking second of it.

I run my hand over my face and try to focus on anything else while DJ takes his turn holding our girl while she sleeps.

Sleep. That's what I'm calling it. The doctor's keep saying a coma. I might be in denial but I can't say those words. I couldn't say them with Lyric without the words dying in my throat. I can't say them with Mariah without my heart feeling like it's going to stop beating.

I close my eyes and rest my forehead against the cool glass. I don't care what any of them say. I still feel like this entire thing is my fault. I went against all of my instincts and played things slow enough with her that she felt like I didn't want her. That DJ and I *didn't want* her. It was my decision. One that DJ followed because he loves and trusts me.

When she started hanging out with Camden, though, we should have made our intentions clear. I don't know what the fuck held me back from doing it. It's not at all like me. Fear? Fuck. Maybe. I've been with DJ so long that even though I felt a connection right away to Mariah, I was afraid to change things. I don't want to fuck anything up. And in trying not to make a mess of things, I created the fucking storm that we're all reeling from.

My eyes snap open when I feel fingers running through my hair. DJ. I look back out the window, not wanting him to see me wallowing.

But I really should know DJ by now.

"You know, if you don't stop blaming yourself for this, I'll have no choice but to take you over my knee," he says quietly. "I might only have one arm, but I can still make good use of the other one." There's a teasing tone to his voice, but it's the dominance that makes me smile and chuckle a little bit as I look at the sling on his arm. Thankfully, nothing broke. But he's still supposed to keep it immobilized for four to six weeks. Something about a nerve.

"I'm bigger than you," I rumble with a half-smile.

"Taller maybe. Bigger dick. But I have more muscles. I could take you."

My smile widens because he knows he can't. I train the cops we work with in defensive tactics and weapons because I'm really fucking good at what I do. I'm a commander with the SWAT team because I know my shit. DJ has tried to take me down many times, in play of course, but hasn't quite been able to manage it yet.

Then again, I guess I don't know that for a fact. The only time he's really been up against me is in training. How would it look to others if anyone was able to take their trainer down? Not to say that none of them can't do it. If they're performing their training moves correctly, I allow the takedown because it means their learning. But if it's something I can get out of, and they can't counter me, I use it for a teaching moment.

After all, there are some people in this world who can outmaneuver a cop. What better way to teach cops how to counter those people than by using someone who can outmaneuver them to train them instead? Seems like a win-win in my book.

DJ sits down in the nook next to me. He wraps his good arm around my waist and kisses me. "So? What's got you in your head today?"

I smile weakly before looking back out the window, then down at my hands. "I really wish I'd just listened to you and told her straight out."

"Baby, come on. You read the situation correctly. If we'd come on that strong, we'd have scared her away. The only reason Camden got close is because he did exactly what we did. Only he asked her out and played a different angle. He made her feel like he was interested without straight out saying it. With us, we made her feel like a friend. But the truth is, Matt, that she needed a friend. Friends. She needed us. Would this have happened if we'd done things differently? I don't know. But my instincts say yes. You saw just how obsessed he seemed to be with her that first day. The way we went about things made our relationship stronger. She trusts us. She loves us. It might not seem like it, but we did it the right way."

I let out a breath. "I know you're right, DJ," I say quietly. "It's just not easy making all of me believe it."

"Then stop listening to your head and listen to your heart instead." DJ leans his head against my cheek. I smile and lean into him as I look at him. He leans in and kisses me. I love the feel of his lips on mine. I have ever since our first kiss.

"Mmm…"

My eyes snap towards Mariah as DJ whips around to look at her. We're both shocked to see her still lying so still. Kieran grunts and starts to sit up. Luca jerks awake. His eyes fly to Lyric. I furrow my brows.

"Lyric?" Kieran asks quietly, rubbing his eyes.

I'd say we're lucky that we got the same room, but luck had nothing to do with it. I would have gone directly to the hospital CEO if I had to. This is not a time to be separated. Even after Mariah had been released, a lot of our time was spent in this room waiting for Lyric. Yesterday was the first day we'd taken a break. A real one.

Lyric's mouth falls open, and she moans. "Oooh…" Her eyelids flutter.

"Shit," DJ rumbles with wide eyes. He takes my hand and leads me to her bed. Kieran sits up as we sit on Mariah's next to her, our hands still linked.

I rub my chest with my other hand as we watch. She's done this once before but never fully came back to us. I'm really hoping she wakes up this time, but the thought of her not makes me anxious.

Kieran takes her hand and rubs his thumbs over her fingers. Luca sits on the other side of her and does the same thing. Kieran kisses her fingers tenderly, one by one, before he holds her hand against his cheek and rubs it against his stubble.

"Mmm… Kier…an…," Lyric whispers. DJ and I share a look. This is more than we've gotten before.

"That's right, baby," he says softly. "I'm here. I'm right here." He kisses her fingers again and holds her hand tighter.

Her eyes flutter open and meet his. Kieran is the first thing she sees, and even I can tell it makes her happy. Her eyes shine with love for him, even though they're a little bit on the confused side and slightly dull from being out for so long.

She moves just a little, like she's trying to sit up. Luca instantly is at her side helping her after pushing a button for the doctors to come in.

But Lyric's eyes never leave Kieran's. I can't help but hope that's how Mariah looks at us when she wakes up. With that much hope, love, and adoration.

"I… dreamt you were… naked… Why aren't you naked?" she asks Kieran. We all laugh.

"What is wrong with you?" Kieran teases as he laughs. "You're unconscious for a fucking week and all you can think about is me naked?"

She giggles as she tries to get comfortable. And then her brain catches up to her. Her eyes widen. "Wait…" She looks around the room and at each of us. When she sees Mariah in the bed next to her, she squeaks and tries to lunge for her. "Oh my God! What happened?" Her monitors start going haywire just as a nurse and doctor come in. They rush to her.

Kieran and Luca both help to calm her as she tries to fight the doctors off to get to Mariah. DJ and I both turn to each other. I wrap my arms around him. He wraps his good arm around me. We both hug each other as tightly as we can, finding comfort and strength in the embrace.

After a few moments, Lyric is calm enough to allow the doctor to do whatever it is he needs to do. My mind is only barely on what anyone in the room is saying. I try to focus, but I can't. I really just want our girls to be okay. And I selfishly hope that Lyric doesn't have some kind of amnesia. I need her to remember everything so it can be one extra nail in Camden's coffin.

I don't know how long the doctor stays in the room answering questions from Luca, Kieran, and DJ. I sit quietly because I don't have a clue what to say or ask. I'm not in cop mode. I'm in boyfriend mode. Brother mode.

I sigh and put my head in my hands, resting my elbows on my knees. This shit can't end fast enough. I'm done wasting time. I want my man and woman by my side. DJ and I waited to get married because we wanted to feel that completion. While we love and are very happy with each other, the ultimate goal has always been feeling the completion. Reaching that unreachable love we've only ever felt with each other.

"Mattie?" Lyric says softly.

I rub my bloodshot eyes and look up at her. "Yeah, sweetheart? How do you feel?"

She shrugs and crooks her finger at me. I realize everyone else but me is surrounding her. Even DJ is sitting on the edge of her bed. I chuckle and stand. I move to her side. I sit next to Luca and lean down. I kiss her forehead as she hugs me.

When I sit back up, she narrows her eyes and flicks my forehead. "Stop that."

"Hey!" I look down at her, amused, as I rub my forehead. "What the hell was that for?"

"You're in your head. You're doing the blaming yourself thing and taking it all on your shoulders. You may be a big guy, Matthew Chance, but you aren't Thor or something."

"You're right. I'm not." I grin and puff up my chest. DJ and I were given scrubs after we were cleared to leave. They gave us some soap to clean up because we had soot and smoke all over us. I had been wearing a Captain America shirt, but we both threw all of our clothes away after we changed. "I'm Captain America."

She playfully swats me, though it's a lot weaker than it usually would be. She giggles a little bit as she smiles. "You're not as hot as Thor."

I grin even wider. "You're right about that, too. I'm hotter."

"Okay, I'll give you that. But Loki's still hotter."

I laugh. "In your dreams, maybe." I lean down and kiss her forehead again. Luca and Kieran hold her hands.

DJ rubs her thigh. "So, what do you remember?" he asks quietly. "I know you told the doctor a little bit, but you held back. We all could see it."

She looks down and nibbles her lip. Kieran runs his thumb over it. She takes a deep breath and looks up at us all. Her eyes flash, and her voice lowers. "I remember everything."

I raise an eyebrow. Internally, I'm elated. "Everything?"

Lyric turns to me. Her eyes, while filled with tears, are dark and angry. "Yeah. Everything. I pushed him away from Mariah. He was hurting her. He was holding her arm hard. He took me in the pool with him at the last second. I remember hitting my head on the edge of the pool. I was woozy but still awake. I couldn't move, though. It was like my body just went into immediate shock. He shoved me away from him. Then I started going under. I tried to fight to get back to the surface, but my body wouldn't obey. It was almost like I was trapped within myself. I didn't start to lose consciousness until I was under the water. I saw him smirking and watched him get out of the pool. He left me there to drown."

"Baby, fuck," Kieran rumbles, swallowing hard. He leans down and wraps his arms around her. "His friends were beating the hell out of me. I couldn't get to you or Mariah."

"What happened before, Lyric? Do you remember?" DJ asks, almost pleadingly. Luca brings her hand to his lips and kisses it in encouragement as Kieran hugs her.

Lyric sniffles as she hugs Kieran the best she can with one hand. "It's okay, my heart," she whispers. "It's okay." After a few moments and some whispering between the two that I can't hear, Lyric takes another deep breath. "His friends were being assholes and splashing around. One of them saw me and Kieran close to Mariah. So, he splashed. He got all of us including Mariah. And then he did it again. He soaked us all and Mariah's laptop."

"And it sparked, which started the fire," I finish.

Lyric nods. Kieran hugs her tighter as she continues. "It must have shocked her or something or burned her because she jumped up and dropped the laptop. Which started the fire on the chair. She got scared. Camden didn't even try to comfort her. He was trying to keep me and Kieran away. He ripped us both away from her. His friends got out of the pool and pushed us both further back from her. He was screaming at her about allowing Kieran to touch her and saying she was his. How he doesn't share."

"And that's when the fight between Kieran and his friends started?" I ask. It's all stuff we already know because of Kieran, but we need to get her corroboration of the entire event.

"I know Kieran was fighting them, but that's when I shoved Camden away from her. She was scared and trying to get away from the fire. You know how she is with fire." Lyric shakes her head. "That was when he pulled me into the pool with him."

I look up at a knock on the door. "Cap?" Tanner says, poking his head in.

DJ squeezes Lyric's thigh as we both stand. "Yeah, Ryan. Come in."

He closes the door gently behind him and sighs when he sees Mariah. "I was hoping they'd both be awake."

"Me too," I say. "At least we got one of them back." I swallow the lump rising in my throat.

Tanner squeezes my arm as he looks at DJ. "Did I give you enough time to question her? Gather the pieces?"

"Yeah. Thanks for holding back." DJ rubs his temple. "I'm going to fucking nail his ass to the wall for this shit."

"He's not going anywhere. I got the DA to ask for no bail. It's going before a judge hard on abuse and stalking, so she thinks she'll get it."

I raise an eyebrow. "How does she know who it's going to be for already? The sun has barely risen."

Sergeant Ryan nods towards Lyric. "Her uncle may have pulled a few strings. It's why he's not here right now."

I chuckle. Her uncle, meaning Chief King, our Chief of Police, would do anything for his niece. Including waking up a judge to gain more sway. Corruption? Probably. But anyone who asks me if I care will get a resounding no because it's my family involved here.

My life.

As Tanner goes over everything with Kieran and Lyric, DJ and I sit down on either side of Mariah. We each take one of her small, frail hands in ours and kiss it.

"Come back to us, baby," DJ rumbles against her fingers.

"You're stronger than you know, sweet girl," I whisper. I lean down and kiss her cheek, still holding her hand. "Fight, baby. Come back to us."

Maybe it's wishful thinking, but I swear she squeezes my hand. I look down at her tiny fingers. Even if it was just in my head, I'm holding onto that. It's one of the only two things getting me through right now.

Her and DJ.

Chapter Thirteen

✫ Mariah ✫

The floor is hot. So, so hot. Why? It's carpet. It shouldn't be so hot. I look down.

No. It's not carpet. At all.

It's concrete. Why is it concrete?

So, so hot.

I try to get up. The flames all around me aren't doing what they do. They're not licking up the wall or across the ceiling. They're not dancing over the floor. Not devouring everything in their path. They're coming for me. Like they're jumping off the walls at me. Diving down from the ceiling trying to get me. Slithering across the floor just for me.

I have to get up. I have to run.

I manage to get to my hands and knees. So, hot.

Burning.

I glance to my left just as the flames fly towards me.

Whispering

What is it saying?

My eyes widen when I see a face in the flames. He's on fire. It's a face of fire. In the fire?

"Ah!" I scream and dive to the ground. It flies over me, still whispering. I look to my right. It should be there.

He should be there.

"Die!" it whispers again. Only this time, I can't see it.

I look all over the place.

The flames are cackling. Laughing at me.

The ground is so hot.

I cry because I know I'm not getting out alive.

"Die!" the voice whispers again. The flames are getting closer. Hotter.

"Ah!" I scream again. Only this time, I don't move. I want to, but I can't. My body is frozen in fear.

Just like it was when I was a kid.

When the flames were chasing me then.

When I was trying to get away and find my dad.

The smoke was so black. Thick. I couldn't find the door to my bedroom. But then I saw an orange glow. I crawled to it. It was so hot and getting hotter the closer I got, but I knew that was my way out. I had to get to the light.

It was so dark.

Just like it is now. All I can see now are the flames wisping towards me. Coming for me. Trying to engulf me in them.

But I still can't move. Just like then. When I got to the door that night, I couldn't reach the door handle because I couldn't get up. I realized that the orange glow was fire. That's why it was so hot. So bright. I managed to back away a little bit, but then my body wouldn't go anymore.

"Mariah!" my dad called just before the door slammed open. "Mariah!"

I heard him.

But I didn't see him. I saw the flames behind him. The fire licking up the door. There was no way out. No way we could go back through the door to escape.

We were trapped.

My dad picked me up and ran for the bedroom window. I was coughing. I couldn't breathe. And all I could see were the flames through the black smoke. Crawling across the ceiling; licking up the walls and door; dancing across the floor.

"Help! Up here!" my dad yelled. I could see something red intermixing with the orange flames, making them glow brighter. "Help! Help!"

I wanted to scream. I wanted to turn my head.

But I couldn't.

The flames were coming at us.

Roaring like a train.

All I could do was watch.

Watch the man on fire dancing in the flames and staring at me. Getting closer and closer to me as the flames made their way towards us.

"Die!" he screamed. "Die! Die! Die!"

My dad got us out before the man on fire reached us. The firefighters made it to us.

Not this time. No one is here to help me this time.

This time it's all on me.

"He's gonna get you, Mariah. Get up," my demon rumbles in my head. "Do you want to die like this?"

I want to say no, but I can't. I'm paralyzed. Every single part of me. I can't even blink. The flames are getting closer to me. Hotter. The ground is starting to scorch me.

I'm going to die. All because I can't fight.

Run.

The face in the fire kneels in the flames near the corner of the room. He smirks at me as he turns into a full body apparition.

"Die!" he screams at me as he flies towards me, stopping at the edge of the flames just about to start consuming my body. He lays down on the ground and looks at me, tilting his head.

I can't scream. My heart is racing so fast, that I can hear it over the flames. I can't even hear my demon's voice anymore. My only source of comfort in this whole thing. The man on fire crawls closer, a grotesque smile on his face, as the flames inch towards me. I can feel my insides trembling, begging me to flee, but my body doesn't obey.

"Come back to us, baby."

My heart skips a beat.

DJ? Can it really be him?

The trembling that had been just on the inside moments ago begins wracking through my body. Only this time, I start trembling on the outside, too. Like DJ's words and voice are giving me some type of strength.

Can I really see them again? Can I go back somehow? We're trapped in my apartment. Aren't we? Are they here?

The man on fire continues to stare at me, hissing. But my eyes can move this time. I flick them to the side, looking for Matt and DJ, but don't see them. When I look back at the man on fire, he's inched even closer. I whimper. My body still won't move. I can't scream.

"You're stronger than you know, sweet girl."

Matt.

Suddenly, an ethereal glow settles around me. The fire demon hisses and charges towards me, but can't get through the bizarre barrier surrounding me; bringing me a sense of calm. Peace.

"What's happening?" *I croak out. The paralyzing fear dissipates the longer the glow surrounds me. I can talk. Move. But most of all, I feel safe. Protected, even though the flames are climbing the walls of the barrier.*

DJ and Matt appear next to me, kneeling at my side. They each smile and hold out a hand. I whimper, unsure if I'm imagining them or if they're really here.

"Diiiiiiiiiiieeeee!" *The man on fire shrieks.* "Diiiiiiiieeeeee!" *He lunges at the barrier again and again.*

I scream and close my eyes.

"Fight, baby. Come back to us," *Matt rumbles.*

My eyes fly open when it gets unbearably hot once more. I jump to my hands and knees and grip Matt and DJ, clinging to them and praying they don't disappear. That I'm not imagining them.

The barrier shatters. The man on fire streaks towards me at warp speed shrieking at me.

"Ah!" I scream as my entire body jerks with the force of him slamming into me. "Ah!" My hands fly to my body. I try to fling the fire off of me. "Ah!"

"Mariah!" someone yells as strong arms wrap around me.

"Ah!" I scream again, still trying to get the flames off me so I don't burn alive. "Ah!"

"Mariah!" someone yells as another arm wraps around me.

Tough.

Soothingly.

"Mariah," someone else whispers softly in my ear. A female. She wraps her arms around me and sways with me. The other sets of arms hug me tighter. "Ssh… It's okay, Mariah… You're safe… Focus on my voice… Feel Matt and DJ…," the voice whispers in my ear. "Let yourself feel…"

Matt.

DJ.

My eyes slowly start to focus as I take deep breath after deep breath. My heart is in my throat. I feel it throbbing; beating like an 808 drum in my ears. I take breath after breath as I cling to the three people holding me. The two others with their hands rubbing my arms and legs.

I don't know how long it takes them to calm me down, but I finally start to regain some sense of myself.

But I still smell it.

The burning.

Charring.

I start to cry. My entire body is wracked with uncontrollable sobs as everything about the fire slams into me with a force greater than that of an atom bomb. Camden starting it. Camden trying to kill all of us. Camden shooting at us. The flames. The explosions. Me becoming catatonic. Not knowing where my loves were.

I cling to DJ and Matt as Lyric quietly slides away, reading that I need them without me saying a word. They hug me even tighter with their lips pressed against my neck; someone's fingers tangled in my hair.

"We got you," DJ whispers.

"We've always got you," Matt rumbles against my neck.

They both keep whispering to me as I cry and hug them both, never once letting me go. Never making me feel crazy or needy for needing them to hold me. I know I'm in the hospital again, but I barely even acknowledge the nurses and doctors who have been checking me out. Matt and DJ stay wrapped around me the entire time. I'm grateful to everyone who works around them so they don't have to release me.

(One Day Later)

I honestly never believed that a person could be so tired in a hospital. Honestly. All that can be done is sleep. Maybe a test here or there. At least, that's how it has always been for me. The rest of the time was spent sleeping.

Not this time. This time, I can't seem to get anyone to leave me alone for longer than five minutes. If it's not the doctors, then it's Matt's and DJ's colleagues. Yesterday, Chief King, Lyric's uncle, was here when I woke up. So was Sergeant Ryan. I'm grateful it was them and not just random cops because they saw the entire screaming episode. They saw the real effects of what Camden did.

I found out that Lyric had woken up just before I did. She'd told Chief King and Sergeant Ryan everything that had happened. Sergeant Ryan was here yesterday to ask questions. Chief King had just arrived here as family, not his official capacity.

But it's been others asking me questions. The fire investigator. An arson specialist. Even the apartment management. I'm so overwhelmed with questions that I want to scream. So, when I look up and see DJ coming in with Sergeant Ryan behind him, I almost lose my mind.

"Please don't make me answer more questions," I whisper.

Matt follows Sergeant Ryan, carrying two cups of coffee. He hands one to DJ. "No more questions, baby," he promises. "Tanner has some news. He wanted to deliver it to all of us."

DJ takes his coffee as he sits next to me. Chief King, sitting on the nook by the window, sits up taller. Lyric crosses her legs and blinks adorably. Kieran rubs her back and puts down the book the two were reading together. Luca puts his phone down with a yawn. Matt settles on the other side of me. Sergeant Ryan, or Tanner, as I now know him, takes a folding chair and flips it backwards. He straddles it as he sits down and looks at us all.

"First thing, Camden has been officially charged with First Degree Attempted Murder, Second Degree Attempted Murder, First Degree Arson, and Second Degree Involuntary Manslaughter."

My eyes widen. "Holy shit...," I breathe. I look up at him. "Are you saying...?" I tick off the charges in my head. The Manslaughter one. That wouldn't be tied to us and our case.

Tanner nods and looks at DJ and Matt. "We tied him to Shannon's murder."

I feel Matt sink against me. "Fuck. Thank fuck."

"How?" DJ asks.

"We got a warrant to search his apartment. He had a lot of shit in his closet that not only tied him to Mariah and the fire, but also to Shannon. He was obsessed with her. Under his bed, though, we found photos of her after he'd killed her. But it wasn't just that. There were photos of her tied up. Photos of her fighting him. Photos of him and his friends..." He trails off and clears his throat. "Well, it wasn't good."

"You're saying that they... assaulted her...," Lyric whispers.

"Uh," Tanner begins. "Uh, well. That was part of it. Yes. But it's a lot more disturbing than that. DNA did match Camden. We believe she was killed during what was going on. They got scared. Probably tried to stage it to look like jealousy of other cheerleaders. There are photos of her alive and after she died. Even after the stage. The DA thinks he'll plead guilty to that. But the part that will get him the most time is the premeditated attempted murder of Mariah. That's a life in prison sentence."

"Good," I say. I take a deep breath as Matt's arms wrap around my waist. DJ is in a sling but his free arm is holding me close.

"That's not all. One of his friends actually turned on him and gave us another tip we're looking into involving his little sister. He had been friends with Camden for a long time and had also babysat the little sister as a favor for the parents a time or two."

"I don't like the sound of this...," Lyric murmurs quietly as she curls into Kieran. I don't blame her. I don't either.

Tanner grimaces before continuing. "Turns out that he noticed something had been off with the little sister for a while. He had become suspicious that Camden could have been the cause after she flinched and shrunk away from him. But he had no proof. So, he decided to stay close to try to get some evidence. Keep your enemies close and all that. He never took part in any of the beating or what happened at the pool, but couldn't risk being distanced from Camden."

"Not a bad plan. Ill-thought out, maybe. But it could work," Matt says, shaking his head.

Tanner nods in agreement. "The little sister opened up to him before she came in to be interviewed. He's who helped her come forward. He was also in the interview room with her. She wouldn't do the interview without him. The parents seem to be in shock. They never noticed anything was wrong. I don't want to get too much into detail, but it looks like when he was eighteen and she was ten, he may have done some pretty bad shit to her. We did interview her. She told us some things, but she broke down. We had to stop the interview. She's fourteen now and suggested that it has gone on this entire time."

I gag, catching his drift. Lyric whimpers and sniffles. I shiver. "How gross," I grumble.

"I really want to nail his ass for all of that, too." Tanner reaches over and squeezes my foot. "It's gonna be a long road, Mariah. But I really wanted to give you some good news. All of you, really. You've been through hell these past couple weeks. Even before everything with Camden started happening. I know this whole thing has been really fucking hard."

I feel DJ smile as he kisses my neck. "A hard fought battle that was won. And the prize at the end of the road was the love we've all been looking for."

Matt kisses my shoulder. "The unconditional kind."

I blush. "Our own fairytale. Like Kieran and Lyric have."

Tanner smiles, and everyone in the room talks for a little while more, but my mind is on the two men next to me.

It hasn't been that long. And I never believed in love at first sight. Only in the books I write. They represent the kind of love I've always wanted. The love I deserve. The kind of love everyone deserves. I never believed it existed outside of the pages I filled with letters and words.

But it does. I have it. Maybe I didn't see it over the first couple of weeks since I met them. I desperately craved it, though. It's why I allowed Camden to pull me into his trap. But it didn't take long to realize that he wasn't what I wanted. He's the same type of man I ran from.

But Matt and DJ.

They are love. Real love. They're my passion. My heart. To find that in one man is rare. To find it in two is like being struck twice by lightning while standing in the exact same place. Because lightning doesn't strike the same place twice.

I can prove science wrong, though, because it did with me. I have the proof in the two men swaying with me right now.

The two men who are not only my demon fighters, but also the light to my dark.

The other half of my broken soul.

Chapter Fourteen

☆ DJ ☆

The next day, after both Lyric and Mariah had been released from the hospital, we're all driving back to the apartment complex. Lyric won't ever mention it, but I know she doesn't feel comfortable coming back here. This had been her safe haven. Camden took that sense of protection away from her.

Just like he had Mariah. We know that Mariah's apartment probably has nothing that's salvageable, but we're hoping that our apartment didn't experience too much smoke damage. Maybe it's still livable.

At least until we can move into the house Matt and I closed on while Mariah and Lyric were unconscious. It shouldn't be long. Living here would be a temporary situation. And if our place suffered too much smoke damage, maybe we can stay with Lyric and Kieran. Lyric and Mariah will do a lot better having each other for support and comfort than they would being apart. In the short time they've known each other, they're already incredibly close.

The truck is silent as Matt follows Luca back to the apartment complex. Luca is driving Kieran and Lyric and plans to survey the situation with Lyric's apartment. I'm not going to pretend he won't also be observing her and her reaction when she walks into it again. We all know that when it comes to staying there or not, Luca is the final say. He's Lyric's twin, but there's a reason he's so trusted among all of us. It's because he knows her better than she knows herself. And his number one priority in life is protecting his sister.

I look down at Mariah and hug her closer when she grips my shirt tighter. I kiss her head as I glance out the front window. I'm sitting in the back with her because she needs to be held. With Matt driving, he couldn't exactly wrap around her. And I can't fit in the front with her with the center console in the way. The decision was I'd sit with her in the back. Matt would drive.

We're getting closer to the apartment complex. Mariah isn't even looking. Her eyes have been closed the whole time since we've left the hospital. Her arm has been lying across my dick. Her hand has been gripping my shirt tightly. The closer we get to the complex, the tighter her fist bunches my shirt.

I run my fingers through her hair and hold her closer. She's not the only one in this truck having a hard time going back. There's a vein in Matt's neck that keeps twitching. My chest is tight. It's gonna be hard for us to see what happened. Mariah might just collapse.

But she'll have us for support. We'll all have each other.

Of course, the plans in my head are nothing like the reality of what happens. The second Matt turns into the parking lot, Mariah is on the floor in tears. She clings to my leg and cries into my knee.

"Jesus, baby," I whisper.

Matt parks and turns around. "Mariah?"

I reach down and try to bring her back up on the seat so I can wrap around her, but she cries even harder. "No! Don't make me! Don't make me. I don't want to go in there anymore!"

"Fuck, baby," Matt whispers. He quickly hops out of the truck and opens the door in the back. He reaches in and starts rubbing her back. "Mariah, you don't have to go in there, sweet girl. No one will make you."

"Mariah. Honey, I'm way too big to get on the floor with you. At least come sit in my lap so I can hold you." My heart is completely shattered. I hate seeing her like this.

Matt leans in and kisses her back. "I'll go, baby. I just need to figure out if anything is salvageable. I won't be long." He glances up at me. I can see the pain he feels for her in his eyes as he takes a breath and closes the door.

I shift as much as I can and guide Mariah so she's between my legs. It's the only way I know how to make her feel protected right now. She's terrified to get into my lap. She doesn't have to tell me it's because she can see the complex more. If she's on the floor, she can keep herself as low as possible and see as little as she can. My goal is to make her only see me.

When I have her positioned between my legs, I tangle my fingers in her hair and hunch down as far as I can. My shoulder stings, but I don't care. She's what matters to me. She buries her face in my thigh and hugs my leg. The sobs have slowed. It's how I know I'm doing something right in making her feel safe.

"I can't... I can't live here," she whispers after a few long moments. She takes a deep, labored breath and shakes her head. "I can smell it. See it all happening all over again."

I swallow hard. "I wouldn't force you to come back here if you can't, baby. We'll figure something out. I'll rent a room until we can move into the house we bought."

We'd told Mariah about the house. We told her we weren't playing games. We wanted her to be with us. She lit up like a Christmas tree, but that brightness quickly died as soon as she found out we couldn't move in right away. She's been pretty quiet ever since.

Now I know why.

We thought she'd be able to stay in our apartment if there wasn't any damage. We underestimated just how much trauma this caused. Just how much it reminded her of her past and brought out the PTSD caused by the fire she was in when she was just a child. To this day, she still sees the man on fire. She can be washing dishes and all of the sudden she'll feel like something is behind her. The man on fire.

It doesn't happen often. She's told us she's usually able to fight him off by telling herself she's being ridiculous. Other times aren't that easy. Just like each time she has to fight the demon in her mind off, she comes back from it feeling childish and crazy.

She doesn't understand that the man on fire is a trauma response. She imagined him as a child as she was going through a horrendous experience. In her mind, seeing the man on fire still to this day is her still trying to make sense of all that happened. She may have seen it when she was just a kid, but it doesn't make it any less scary as an adult. Especially since she never had the chance to truly deal with it.

"I c-can't, DJ... I-I'd rather be homeless." Being homeless. Another big trigger for her. One of her biggest fears. She was homeless as a kid. She was a little older than she was after the fire happened, but they lived in a car. She vowed to never be homeless again.

"I'm not letting that happen, baby. I have a backup plan. I always have a backup plan."

And I do. It's who I am. Being a leader in the Army Rangers and a leader as a cop, I always have multiple plans just in case one doesn't work. My Plan B in this case is living with Lyric and Kieran. Plan C, in the event that Lyric can't handle it here, is to stay at her place anyway. Plan D, if Mariah can't handle it here at all, is to move in with Luca. Plan E, in the event that neither Lyric or Mariah can deal with staying, is to move in with Luca. We'd already agreed his place is big enough. His girlfriend doesn't mind. I even had a plan F. If none of the above was an option, we'd planned on moving in with Tanner. He has become a good friend to all of us through this and offered his spare bedroom.

Mariah sniffles. "What's the plan?" she whispers.

I hug her the best I can and kiss her head, keeping my fingers tangled in her hair. I have many more plans involving a good friend of mine, Matt's parents, and his sister, but when I see Luca and Kieran usher a crying and devastated looking Lyric back out to Luca's car, I have to smile a little because I knew in my heart where we'd all end up. I really didn't need more than one plan.

"Plan E, baby. You obviously won't do well here. Even if it wasn't in mine and Matt's apartment and we chose Lyric's two floors down, you wouldn't be able to do this. Lyric doesn't feel safe here either. So, we're all moving in with Luca. He has three bedrooms. His girlfriend is on board. So, we're moving there temporarily."

She nods, but she doesn't relax. She won't until we're driving away. "I have nothing left. I know it. It's all gone. Everything I worked so hard for..."

"Everything can be replaced, baby. We'll start over."

As I watch Matt come out, I know instinctively he feels the same way. We're not grabbing anything we don't need from our apartment. If it smells like smoke, it can stay. Neither of us want the memories to haunt our girl. Even if the clothes can be cleaned, we'll happily donante them if it means she's okay and not traumatized further.

Matt climbs in the truck and turns. He kisses both me and Mariah. "New memories. New life, baby."

Mariah nods. I smile as I meet his eyes. He kisses me again before he turns. He pulls out of the parking lot and follows Luca to his house.

New memories.

New life.

I can't wait.

Chapter Fifteen

☆ *Matt* ☆

(Six Months Later)

Mariah cuddles into my side after setting her soda on the table. She's on a new medication for her anxiety, depression, and panic. Nefazodone. She's doing really well on it but needs to drink soda with it or it makes her dizzy as fuck and tired as hell. Coupled with her therapy, though, Mariah is honestly thriving. She's even stronger than she was six months ago when we first met her. I'm constantly proud of the way she fights each and every day.

"I love this movie," Mariah whispers as she snuggles even closer. I fucking love when she cuddles with us. I love the way she feels against my body. I love even more when she's between me and DJ and screaming our names as she comes.

I kiss her head. "*Shawshank Redemption* is a good movie. One of mine and DJ's favorites."

"I just love how they portray… well, everything. I love how they portray life in prison. How it's so structured. Even the gangs and threats.

The hierarchy among the prisoners. I mean, Red. He's older, but the gang doesn't touch him. They go for the young ones who can fight."

"Probably because the fight turns them on."

"Well, maybe. But I still think it has a lot to do with who he is. It's more than that, though. This movie really shows how prison affects a person and their spirit. It shows the institutionalism that older prisoners feel. Even the younger ones, even though they don't know it. Prison is all they know. So, when they get released they don't know what to do."

I smile, loving how passionate she gets. "They definitely did a good job with it. We see a lot of people who tell us they commit crimes because prison is better than being on the streets. Inside, they know what's happening; what to do. Out here, they're fucking losers and nothing in a world that simply doesn't want to give them a chance. No one likes a convict except gangs and other cons."

Mariah nods. "And there are really only two options. When they come out, especially the older ones, everything is different. Can you imagine someone who went to prison in the seventies and just gets out now? They'd have no idea how to use the internet or what social media is. And if they did, it's not really like they'd get to use it in there. I mean, can you imagine being able to take a picture on your phone and send it instantly to a friend or relative? Just that would be scary. Brooks couldn't handle it. Prison was his home. Out here, he was like an alien in a foreign world."

"First option. Suicide. We see that a lot, unfortunately. Some are suicide by cop because they can't handle it out here."

I hate those kinds of calls. Suicides are hard enough, but a suicide by cop is traumatic on many levels. Not just for the families of the person who did it, but also for us. Especially the cop who may have been forced to pull the trigger. The public always has an opinion. The person was sick. Depressed. You should have called in someone who can work with him and talk him down. Sometimes, that's not an option. We can't wait for someone or talk a person down if they're shooting at us or others.

It's those calls that are the worst. The calls where we know the person needs help and can benefit from the resources we can offer, but we can't get help for them because the situation has escalated to levels we can't come back from. If a person comes out of his house shooting at officers or shooting at nearby houses, we have to think of other people's lives. We'll do all we can before we pull the trigger, including less than lethal options, like tasers or bean bag guns, but we can't allow a killing spree.

"Exactly. The second option is what Red was thinking. Commit another crime to get put back in. He was talking about killing the store manager just so they'd put him back."

"Some are able to manage it," DJ says when he comes back. He leans over and kisses Mariah as he hands me my drink. She closes her eyes and smiles into the kiss. DJ takes the opportunity to let his eyes dart towards the coffee table. He quickly slips a ring over the reusable, silicone straw in Mariah's cup. I grin. When he pulls back, he smiles. "So, that's three options, technically."

Mariah nods. "True. Red found Andy. Did you know there is a lot of curiosity and theories about the ending, though? Some think that Red committed suicide just as Brooks did. That the ending was his Heaven."

DJ shakes his head. "I don't believe that. If that were the truth, they wouldn't have done that whole part where he finds the money and Andy's note. And then his inner dialogue where he says he broke the law for the second time in his life. Meaning the murder he committed as a young man, and then the parole violation where he buys the bus ticket and skips out on his parole. He goes to the same city that Andy crossed the border. From there, he goes to the city Andy told him. And just like Andy said, he'd be there in a house on the beach working on a boat."

"Also true. I just really love this movie." Mariah leans forward as DJ and I watch her closely. She grabs her cup, then cuddles back into us. I casually run my fingers through her hair and play with the ends.

DJ sits back with a grin he's trying like hell to hide. I reach into the bowl of popcorn with M&Ms sitting on my lap after putting my own drink on the table. We both watch as Mariah takes a drink.

Suddenly, she gasps. Her eyes cross. The straw is still in her mouth. Her eyes widen in shock as they dart between the two of us. We both try to keep our eyes on the screen so we don't let on that we're watching her reaction through our peripheral vision, but it proves to be very difficult.

Finally, she squeals. She puts the cup down and slides the ring off the straw. She puts the ring on her finger with wide eyes. "Oh my God!" She launches at me and kisses me deeply. I barely have time to put my arms around her before she's launching at DJ and kissing him just as deeply. "Oh my God!"

"Marry us," DJ murmurs against her lips as I scoot closer.

"Let us treat you like the Queen you are for the rest of our lives," I say, wrapping an arm around her waist, even though she's straddling DJ. I grip her ass.

"Oh my God!" she squeaks again. She leans over and kisses me, then DJ, and then me again. "Oh my God! Oh my God! Oh my God!"

DJ laughs. Mariah jumps off him still squeaking and squealing. She jumps up and down and starts stripping. Mine and DJ's mouth both drop as we watch her. She pushes her panties down at the same time she strips her t-shirt. We watch in fascination as she pulls her bra over her head without undoing it. She tosses it somewhere and jumps DJ. With her ass in the air and knees on the couch, she tugs his sweats down and starts sucking his dick.

"Holy shit, Mariah," DJ moans. His fingers automatically tangle in her hair.

After I finally catch my damn breath at how brazen she is and how fucking turned on I am, I move quickly. I tug down my sweats and position myself behind her. As DJ guides her pace, she bobs her head up and down over and over again, sucking DJ's cock.

I slide in her pussy because I can't fucking resist. "Fuck, sweet girl," I moan as her tight pussy envelops my dick, making me even harder. "Goddamn."

She moans as I start thrusting into her in time with the pace she's sucking DJ. Her pussy pulses around me and clenches tightly. I grip her hips. My eyes can't decide where they want to look. I dart from how sexy DJ looks pumping into her mouth and how sexy she looks taking my cock.

"Jesus, baby. Your mouth," DJ closes his eyes and lets his head fall back against the couch. He thrusts faster into her mouth.

She moans and whimpers around his dick, pushing back into me harder. It's her cue that she needs more. I happily oblige and give her exactly what she's asking me for. I grip her hips a little more firmly and thrust faster, harder, and deeper. I roll my hips against her and shift my hips, thrusting into her at several different angles.

She screams around DJ's dick. I grin when his eyes fly open. He groans low. His hips jerk into her, and I decide that while my dick pounding our girl's pussy is sexy as fuck, watching DJ's reactions to her sucking his cock is even better.

I slam into her again and again. She grips his thighs for balance. He thrusts into her mouth, fucking it uncontrollably. Mariah starts playing with his balls and tugging them with one hand and stroking him with the other. She twists her wrist. Him watching her and panting for her as her pussy gets tighter and tighter for me brings me closer and closer to the edge.

"Christ, baby girl. I'm gonna come." I slap her ass. She screams again. DJ jerks into her once more. Her pussy pulses and clenches erratically. Her thighs tremble. I know she's ready to break.

"Damn, Mariah," DJ groans. When his eyes roll back, I know he's ready, too.

"Come, baby. Come all over my cock," I command.

"Mmm!" Mariah cries out as her walls clamp around me. She comes hard for me, soaking my dick as she quivers and quakes. She slams herself into me just as I bury myself in her.

As her pussy spasms around me, I lose my load deep inside her. "Holy fuck, Mariah!" I shout.

"Ah! Mariah!" DJ yells as his hips jerk while he comes down her throat.

"Mmm!" she screams again.

A few moments later, DJ slowly pulls out of her mouth when he finishes. She collapses against his lap moaning as I slowly pull out of her as well. My come leaks from her pussy, making me moan again. It's fucking sexy to see our girl covered in us.

"So, is that a yes?" I ask, leaning down and kissing her pretty ass.

She looks over her shoulder at me with wide eyes. "You mean I never answered?"

DJ chuckles as I shake my head with a grin. "No, ma'am," DJ drawls. "Here we are trying to figure out if we're engaged or not," he teases.

"Oh my God, yes!" Mariah gets up on her knees and straddles DJ. "Yes! Yes! Yes!" she squeals as she kisses him deeply, wrapping her arms over his shoulders.

I grin and wrap my arms around them both. I kiss the back of her neck. "Fuck, I'm so happy to hear those words."

She turns and kisses me just as deeply as she did DJ. Before I know what's happening, she's slamming down on DJ's cock and riding him hard and fast. She looks up at me submissively, but I know damn good and well what my girl needs. I have no issues filling her pussy with my dick, too.

I straddle DJ and push her forward as I slide my dick in along DJ's inside her wet pussy. DJ and I both wrap our arms around each other and let Mariah get her fill of us.

Over.

And over.

And over.

When we're finally all exhausted enough, we make our way upstairs and fall into bed in a tangle of naked limbs. It's my favorite way to fall asleep and wake up.

I'm beyond ecstatic that I get all of this, them, for the rest of my life.

Chapter Sixteen

☆ Mariah ☆

(Six Months Later)

I smile as the bright Florida sun reflects off the pretty blue sapphire ring on my left ring finger, making it shine. Getting engaged to them six months ago felt more right than anything I've ever done in my entire life.

I haven't heard the demon's voice in almost an entire year. The longer I go without him beating me down, the more confident I start to feel in myself. Lighter. Happier. More free. Like I can breathe without feeling his weight on my shoulders as he holds me down.

Of course the freedom I feel could have something to do with the fact that Camden was convicted of First Degree Attempted Murder. Three counts of it for me, Matt, and DJ. He was also convicted of Involuntary Manslaughter of his ex-girlfriend, Shannon, as well as the attempted murder of Lyric. His friends that were involved in beating Kieran were all convicted of Assault.

But there was one thing that made us all sick. He was also convicted of molesting and sexually assaulting his sister. It came out in trial that he'd been abusing her for years. She turned to his friend, who was the only person she trusted, and told him what was happening when his friend noticed she was hurt one day. The details of what he did to her are disgusting and turn my stomach every time my mind wanders to that subject.

As scary as everything that happened was, there was a lot of good that came out of it all. Matt and DJ had been looking for a house. While I was in the hospital, they closed on one. I had no idea what I was going to do. My apartment had been completely gutted by the fire. The apartment on the other side of me also suffered fire damage. Several others had smoke damage, including Matt's and DJ's.

After Lyric and I were released, we all went back to the apartment together. I couldn't even go in. As soon as Matt turned into the parking lot, I was already crying. I didn't need to see it. I felt it close. I smelled the smoke. By the time he parked, I was curled on the floor of Matt's truck, trembling. DJ stayed in the truck with me. He held me between his legs and kept the apartment building out of my view until Matt came back out.

Nothing in my apartment was salvageable. I lost the entire life I'd built for myself. I felt violated and helpless, the two feelings I'd never wanted to experience ever again. I'd worked hard to be independent, make my own money, and have my own place to myself. Everything I'd done to give myself the life I've never had was gone in an instant.

Camden.

He almost took everything from me. He nearly stole my life.

But he didn't take what matters the most to me. Lyric and Kieran are alive. They both made it through what he did to them. Lyric tried to stay in the apartment she and Kieran lived in, but she couldn't. As soon as they walked in the day we all returned, she was trembling. She attempted to stay strong and not show it, but she broke down when they walked in. Kieran knew instinctively that she didn't feel safe anymore. Luca moved them both into his house that very day.

Camden didn't take Matt or DJ away from me. The three of us have only grown closer by the day. They are the part of me I didn't really know was missing when Camden tried to steal from my life. While they are still just as much that today, they've also become my whole world.

It's kind of funny when a person finds their soulmate, or in my case, soulmates. I didn't expect it. Looking back, I was completely swept off my feet by both Matt and DJ. Neither of them even had to say a word. I don't know where my head was at over the two weeks I allowed Camden in my life. The only thing I can really think of is that he paid attention to me and was very upfront that he liked me. While my heart was always with Matt and DJ, they never expressed that interest. At least not like Camden did. Not as boldly.

Because the truth is, Matt and DJ had expressed interest. They weren't as in my face about it, but they spent a lot of time with me. Everything they did over those couple of weeks showed me how much they cared and how interested they were. I still haven't completely forgiven myself for not seeing it. It was time wasted. Time that was so close to ending.

A low growl emits from the large, black furry creature who puts his large head in my lap. I look down at Loki, my purebred wolf. "May I help you?"

He looks up at me with his pretty brown eyes and flicks his tongue out. It's his way of stopping me from getting too deep in my thoughts. It was about a month after the fire when we moved into the house. I love it. It's large, but the best part is the backyard. It's peaceful and big. A good enough size that the wolves we have are happy. They have a lot of room to run.

With Matt and DJ going back to work, I'd been left home alone. It only took a week for them to come home with Loki. And three other adorable wolves. Loki's brothers and sisters. Loki and I took an immediate attachment to each other.

Funnily enough, the other wolves did the same. Tyr is absolutely Matt's. She's a pretty snow white wolf. Valkyrie took to DJ very quickly, but she's the most shy of all of them. She's white, gray, and brown, the perfect mix of all of her brothers and sisters. Magni is a gorgeous gray wolf. He took to Lyric right away. Which was good because she fell in love with him.

A couple of months after we moved in, the house next door came up for sale. Lyric and Kieran bought it and moved in. Until then, Magni was a reserved wolf and watched out for everyone, wolf and human alike. He still does, but Lyric is simply his.

We took the fence separating our yards down and turned it into one large property with our own houses. I love that they're so close. They've been like family to Matt and DJ for a while, but it didn't take long for me to think the same way about them. We're all ecstatic we're all close and together, and the wolves are even more happy that they aren't separated, even though Magni refuses to leave Lyric's side. He doesn't live with us anymore. The wolves didn't know what to make of that, but they all seem happy knowing he's close.

"Cannon ball!" Layne, DJ's adopted nephew, bellows as he sails through the air and hits the water. Layne is DJ's best friend's son.

"Eek!" Lyric screams as she flails and falls in the pool chair next to me. I swear Magni chuckles as he sits next to her and watches Layne.

"Another cannon ball!" Beckett, Matt's nephew and Layne's boyfriend, yells as he flies through the air and makes another big splash.

I laugh as Tyr and Valkyrie follow them. Lyric giggles as she settles. Kieran grins as he lights the grill on our large, connected patio. Matt and DJ come out of the house in their shorts and leap into the pool with the boys, where an immediate splashing fight occurs.

Everyone laughs as we all relax in each other's company. It's like music to my soul, and I'm so happy to say *this* is my life.

☆☆☆

Later that night, after everyone has gone home and the wolves are settled, I lean against the doorframe of our bedroom biting my lip. A smile dances across my face, and I lean my head against the wall as I hug myself.

"Fuck, DJ," Matt moans. I can see his eyes roll back in his head from here. His back arches, and he slams his ass back into DJ.

"Ah, hell, Matt. How do you feel this damn good after all these years?" DJ groans.

I lick my lower lip and cross my legs. I swallow down the moan threatening to escape because I really like watching my men together. DJ's hard, thick dick slamming into Matt's ass is real life porn I never knew I needed. I don't even have to touch myself. I'm already on the edge of coming. The two are sexy and hot with their clothes on, but when they take them off, I'd drop to my knees and beg for them if they asked me to.

I shift a little and lick my lip again wondering how I got so lucky. Matt meets each of DJ's thrusts. DJ's cock disappears in Matt's ass again and again. But it's when DJ reaches down and starts stroking Matt's dick that my knees get weak.

I have two vices. The first is watching DJ or Matt get each other off. The second is one of them fucking the other while I suck their lengths. I love the taste of them. I just really love them. I've fallen so far and so deep. They treat me like a woman should be treated. And I treat them like the Kings they are.

DJ grunts. "Damn, I'm gonna come." DJ throws his head back as he slams his dick into Matt one last time. "Oh, fuck! Matt!" He never stops stroking Matt's dick. Matt groans and drops his head. I know he's trying to hold back, but it isn't easy when DJ feels as good as he does. I know all too well.

"DJ, I'm so fucking close," Matt moans as he grips the comforter underneath him.

DJ groans and jerks his dick into Matt one last time before he pulls out. He grips Matt's hips and flips him over onto his back as he leans down and starts sucking. I give myself a mental pat on the back for not jumping into the fray and sucking Matt off myself so he came at the same time as DJ. If I didn't like watching so much, I probably would have.

Moments after DJ starts sucking Matt's dick, Matt damn near howls as he comes. "Holy shit, DJ!" His hips arch off the bed and jerk erratically as DJ swallows every last delectable drop.

I finally let out the moan I've been holding in. "My God. Why do I always have to show up at the most inopportune times?" I tease with a sultry smile. I can't seem to look at anything other than their dicks. They both look at me with huge smiles that make my panties melt right off. If I were wearing any. Which I'm not.

DJ pulls away from Matt, releasing his dick with an audible pop that makes Matt jump and moan. "Come over here so we can bury ourselves in you," DJ drawls.

"Hmm… Haven't you boys had enough?" I raise an eyebrow.

Matt laughs and crooks his finger at me. "We could never have enough. Of you or each other."

I blush as I make my way towards the bed. I'm only wearing one of DJ's t-shirts. Nothing else. I can already feel myself dripping down my thighs in anticipation of what's to come. I love their fingers. Their tongues are deadly. But neither of that is what I want tonight. A year ago, I may have been afraid to ask or tell them my desires.

No more.

They've given me some of the confidence and strength I knew was dormant underneath all the layers. I'm sure I haven't scratched the surface of what I could become with the amount of support I get from them and the family I found in Lyric, Kieran, and Luca.

I feel the blush in my cheeks rush down my entire body when I see them both watching me hungrily. Their eyes seemingly glow with all of their longing. Goosebumps erupt on my skin the closer I get to them. I can feel the heat in their expressions.

I pull the t-shirt over my head as I reach the side of the bed. Matt moves up and sits up, leaning against the headboard as DJ cleans himself up. I watch them shyly. DJ takes my hand after tossing the wet wipe he was using into the trash by the bed and kisses it as he guides me into the bed. Matt's hand finds my ass.

"You're dripping for us," DJ rumbles, his eyes traveling down my body and stopping on my pussy. He licks his lips, and I shiver.

I feel Matt's finger slide along my pussy from behind as DJ watches. I shudder. "Oh God," I whisper. I steady myself on Matt's perfectly sculpted abs.

"Definitely wet and ready," Matt says with a smirk as he brings his finger to his lips and sucks me off him. I both blush and whimper.

DJ grins. "God, those sexy sounds you make, baby. They're going to be my undoing." He helps me straddle Matt.

Matt's hands automatically find my hips as he positions me over his already hard cock. My back is to him, but I don't need to see him to know his eyes are sparkling with anticipation. I grip DJ's shoulders as Matt's throbbing dick spears me when he drops me over him. We both groan in unison while DJ watches Matt enter me.

"Oh God, Matt," I moan. "Sometimes I forget how big you are."

"Well, I'm happy to remind you, ma'am," Matt drawls in an overly exaggerated Southern accent that still brings me to my knees and makes my pussy throb.

DJ rumbles approvingly at how good I take Matt. He leans forward and rubs the head of his cock through my wetness, making my eyes flutter closed. I feel the heat from his body when he inches closer.

"Whose good girl are you?" he whispers in my ear. His warm breath tickles my neck, making me shudder and gasp. Matt's lips brush across my shoulder as his arms encircle my waist.

I love how big these two are compared to me. I feel like they could engulf me completely. I've never felt so loved and safe with anyone as I do with them. I trust them implicitly. Probably since I first met them, but it wasn't until after the fire that we all had a serious conversation about where we stand. It was the best talk I'd ever had because everything was laid out on the table. We all knew what we wanted.

Eternity with each other. Our very own forever and always.

"Yours. Always yours," I whisper.

DJ grips my hips as I settle against Matt's chest. My eyes roll back at the new position and how Matt fills me even more. DJ grips my ass. My eyes fly open when I feel him start to enter me.

"Oh!" My pussy spasms. I jerk into him, nearly coming.

"Fuck, baby." DJ kisses me deeply, his tongue dancing with mine, as Matt rumbles against my neck and kisses it.

Vibrations rock through my body. My pussy pulses erratically; needy for them. The deeper DJ slides into me, the closer I get to losing all control right here and now. I grip his arms as Matt hugs me tighter. DJ kisses down my neck as he braces himself with one hand against the headboard. The other grips me more firmly.

Matt moans. "Christ, you're so tight."

I want to say it's just that their dicks are so big, but all that comes out of my mouth is a sigh, a moan, and unintelligible mumbling. They're so deep. So hard. So big. When just one of them is inside me, I'm skyrocketed straight to Heaven's door. When they're both inside me, just like this, they take me beyond Heaven to some realm that has no name.

"Fuck…," I finally murmur as my pussy pulses erratically. "I'm not going to last long." My nails dig into DJ's back when I wrap my arms around him, pulling him closer. I love feeling like I'm being crushed between them. I wrap my legs around his waist just as tightly as my arms are.

"Me either with how fucking tight you are and the feel of Matt's dick against mine." DJ smiles against my neck as they both start slowly thrusting inside me.

"Oh…, Mariah," Matt groans against the other side of my neck. "My God, baby girl." His arms tighten around me. His lips move off my neck at the same time DJ's do. My head falls against Matt's shoulder as his lips meet DJ's in a hot kiss that makes me wetter for them.

As their tongues dance, they thrust into me harder, deeper, and a little faster. I tighten around them with each thrust. My pussy clenches and pulses. My thighs tremble. My stomach quivers. I don't want to come yet. It feels too good. I buck into them, meeting their thrusts. I moan and turn towards them just as they break from each other and start devouring me. Matt keeps one arm around me and wraps his other one around DJ, pulling him even closer.

"Oh…," I moan, kissing them just as hungrily. DJ, his hand still gripping my ass, pulls me into his thrusts. They both thicken inside me.

"You're gonna have to come for us, sweet girl," DJ rumbles. "We're both about to fill that pretty pussy of yours."

Matt slides his hand slowly to my clit. He cups my pussy and pulls me into his thrusts as he rubs my clit. They both pump in and out of me. As soon as his thumb touches my sensitive flesh, I'm careening off the peak of the high they've driven me too. My pussy clenches tight around them and spasms as I come, soaking their dicks and my thighs.

"Ah! Matt! DJ!" I shout. My hips jerk as uncontrollably as my pussy pulses for them.

"Oh, Mariah…, baby. DJ…," Matt groans as he slams inside me one last time, burying his dick in my pussy.

"Fuck! Mariah! Matt!" DJ moans as he pounds into my pussy once more before burying himself deep inside me.

True to their word, they come hard inside me at the same time, filling my pussy with jet after jet of their come. I take it all with gasp after gasp, holding DJ as close to me as I can, staying wrapped around him. DJ's arm drops from the headboard and wraps around Matt's shoulders. We all stay tangled with each other panting as we come down.

Several minutes later, after we're finally able to move enough to drag ourselves to the bathroom and clean up, the three of us crawl into bed naked. Matt and DJ tuck me between them. We all snuggle as close as possible.

We've come so far in just a year, but I know I want to spend the rest of my life with them. They're my light; my saviors when I'm sinking.

They're what makes my heart beat. Being with them is so different than any other person I've ever been with. I don't question their love or my love for them.

As we fall into a deep, exhausted sleep, I let their love wrap the familiar blanket of peace around me. I surrender to it and sink into them.

My heart and soul.

Epilogue

☆ DJ ☆

(Six Months Later)

I lean over the back of the oversized chair in our beachfront suite and kiss my wife's neck with a smile. "Hey, beautiful."

"Hi." Mariah smiles as she looks up at me. "I was just enjoying the sunrise. Thought I'd get some writing in. I felt inspired."

I grin and wrap her in a hug from behind. I press my cheek against hers and read what she's typed. It took her almost this whole year to get back into writing. After we moved into Luca's, we bought a few things we'd need while we were waiting to move into our house. Things like clothing and other necessities. We made sure we got Mariah copies of her identification as well as a new laptop. They were two things that she was extremely anxious about. She didn't seem to care about anything else except making sure she could identify herself and write if she felt like she needed to. Writing has always been a way to ground herself. It's why she has so many books out.

But she didn't touch the laptop until just a couple of weeks ago. Right before we got married. She hadn't even taken it out of the box. Matt and I got home after work and she was sitting on her chair in the corner of the room with the wolves curled around her at her feet. She was so into her writing, she didn't even know we'd come in. Turns out, she'd woken up inspired and wrote nearly an entire book by the time we got back.

I kiss her neck as I start reading what she's written out loud. "'No one can save me now but you,' he says. He sinks to his knees, clinging to me. He falls to the ground on his side. Blood intermixes with the water under him. The rain pours over him, quickly washing the blood seeping from his side down the street in the storm drain. His guards bark orders. Someone rushes to his side. All of the chaos seems to fade away until all that exists is me and him. I don't even realize the animalistic scream piercing my eardrums is me." I hiss out a breath through my teeth. I'm in awe of my girl. "Fuck me, baby. What the hell are you writing?"

She turns to me and smiles. "It's a mafia romance. The main character just got gunned down in the street as he and his girl were getting in the car. I'm almost to the end of the book."

"Shit. Tell me he survives."

"Well, of course he does. He's the mafia boss. I can't kill him off."

I laugh. "Well, you probably could. But you'd break a lot of your reader's hearts."

"I've done that before."

I laugh again. "I don't doubt that. I constantly hear you talking about how a book is so good, but you're bawling your eyes out and telling me how it broke you."

She giggles as she closes her laptop and puts it on the end table. I move in front of her and kneel in front of her, taking her hands. I kiss them both, then kiss her palms. She smiles down at me and shifts so she can kiss my head.

"The best books are the books that break you and put you back together. Case in point? Any book by Tracy Lorraine or Leila James. Two of my favorite authors."

"Says the girl with an entire bookshelf at home filled with every single book either of those authors have ever written."

She laughs. "Where's Matt? I like him better. You're just mean to me."

I give her a wicked grin. "Really? I'm mean to you?" I lean down and kiss her bare thigh as I let go of her hands. I let my fingertips wander up her thighs until I reach her panties. I run a thumb down her center over her panties. She's already nice and damp. "Pretty sure your pussy doesn't think I'm mean."

She gasps and lets her head fall back when I press my thumb over her clit. "Oh, DJ… Okay, you're right. I love you. You're not mean to me."

I grin and push her panties aside. "That's my girl." I waste no time diving into her pussy with my tongue.

"Ah! DJ!"

"I love the way you taste. Like a fucking vanilla latte mixed with you." I thrust my tongue into her. Hard.

"Oh!" She grips my hair and pulls me closer as she moans. Loudly. I love making her make the sounds she does.

"Mmm…," I growl into her pussy. She jerks into me. Her pussy clamps around my tongue and pulses. I thrust faster, as deeply as I can, while I swirl my tongue inside her.

"Oh…, DJ…" She arches into me. Her thighs are already trembling, and I haven't even started yet.

I nip and nibble her pussy. She gasps and moans, riding it uncontrollably as I twist, swirl, and crook it inside her. I suck on her pussy. I haven't even touched her clit yet, but I know when I do, she'll completely unravel for me. She's already so close.

I lick from her pussy to her clit, but hold back from sucking her little bundle of nerves. It elicits a sexy as fuck moan as she arches into me once more. Keeping her panties pushed aside, I slowly thrust just one finger inside her. I turn it just enough so when I start crooking it, I'll hit her spot.

"Best breakfast ever," I moan against her clit. The vibration of my voice against her makes her writhe for me. I start sucking her clit and flicking my tongue over it just as I start crooking.

"Ah! DJ! Oh fuck, yes!" She arches uncontrollably and pulls me as close to her pussy as possible. I'm happy to bury my face in her if it means making her come.

Like she's just about to.

Her pussy clamps hard around my finger. I can feel her starting to spasm as she moans. Her hips jerk. I nip her clit, causing her to scream.

Usually, I give the command to come, but not this time. I want her to lose control; to wait until she can't hold it back anymore.

"Fuck, DJ... DJ! I'm gonna... I'm gonna... Ah! I'm gonna come!" she shouts. I don't stop. I keep crooking against her spot and sucking her clit as I lick and flick my tongue over it. I growl possessively, and it's all it takes. "Ah! DJ!" She jerks into my mouth again and again as her pussy walls collapse. She comes hard, soaking my finger.

I grin and lick my way from her clit down to her pussy. "Holy fuck, beautiful. You're incredible." I slowly remove my finger and lick her clean, gently bringing her down from her high.

My dick is straining against my boxer briefs. It's all I'm wearing, and I completely regret throwing them on when I woke up this morning and Mariah wasn't in our arms. I don't know how the fuck she got out of bed without either of us waking up. Must have been because we were so tired after our fuck fest last night in celebration of our wedding night.

We were married in an intimate union ceremony on the beach in the Florida Keys just yesterday. It was beautiful. Mariah looked incredible in her long, white, and very light dress. Her long hair was swept into a pile on her head that somehow looked fucking incredible. Matt and I wore white to match her. We each had a pink carnation in our lapels because pink is her favorite color and the carnation is her favorite flower.

Kieran, Lyric, Chief King, Tanner, my nephew, Layne, and Matt's nephew, Beckett, were all here to witness our union. Matt's parents and sister were here. Layne's dad, a Sergeant with Gainesville P.D. and my best friend was here. We didn't want a big wedding. We just wanted close friends and family with us. After the ceremony, we all had dinner and danced a little bit before going our separate ways.

The three of us made love all night long. We were insatiable and couldn't get enough of each other. I have a feeling it's going to be like that the whole time we're on this honeymoon. We have a lot of plans, including a cruise, but in actuality, we really don't need any of them. We're content in this room with each other.

"Are you two having fun without me?" Matt asks. We both turn towards him. He's grinning.

I lick my lips. "Even in the morning after taking loads of come, she tastes like a fucking latte. How's that possible?"

Matt stalks towards us, his grin widening. His dick is hard. He was smart enough to not wear boxers. "I'm pretty sure it's just the way she tastes. Unique to her."

Mariah blushes as I stand, pulling off my boxers. "You two are so attractive. It's just unfair. You should honestly arrest each other."

We both laugh as Matt leans down and kisses her. He lifts off her shirt as he pulls away. "What do you think, baby? After last night, do you think you can take us both?"

She blushes. "Does it make me insane if I say yes, considering how many times you both made me come last night?"

I take one of her hands as Matt takes the other. "I'd say that makes you human. You just want your husbands and love how good we feel," I say as we pull her up. I strip her panties off and kiss her pussy as I stand.

Matt leans down and grips her upper thighs. He picks her up. She wraps her legs around his waist and arms around his shoulders. I love Mariah's curves. She's all woman and naturally beautiful. She hates makeup so she never wears it. She's so self-conscious about her body because just a few years ago she weighed over three-hundred pounds. I've seen pictures. I think she was just as beautiful then, but she has a hard time believing me. Matt feels exactly the same.

Matt stands in the middle of the room kissing our girl. She's wrapped tightly around him. Stroking my cock, I make my way behind them. I push Mariah's gorgeous, silky hair off her shoulder and press my lips against her neck. I let my hand trail down her body and relish in the goosebumps I leave in my wake.

"God, you're beautiful," I rumble against her neck while Matt steals her breath.

"Mmm...," she moans.

I reach down and grip Matt's dick. I stroke it a few times. His deep moan makes my cock twitch. I lick a finger and slide it through Mariah's wetness, dipping it into her pussy. She sighs in pleasure. Her head falls back against my shoulder. I let Matt lick her off my finger as I guide us both to her pussy.

"Fuck, you're right," Matt rumbles when he's finished licking her off me. He leans forward and kisses her neck. "She does taste like a latte."

"Oh...," she moans. She arches as Matt and I both start pushing into her. We've never taken her like this before. Standing up like this.

"I can't make it to the couch. I need you, baby," Matt says, echoing my own thoughts.

"Don't… stop…" She writhes and arches between us. She grips Matt tighter with her legs and reaches behind her to wrap her arms around my shoulders.

"Don't plan to," I rumble against her neck. I kiss and nibble it, then kiss up to her jaw. She turns her head so I can kiss her.

Matt and I thrust deeper and deeper into her. I kiss her, tangling my tongue with hers. Matt keeps her firmly situated between us. I wrap my arms around his shoulders. Mariah opens more and more for us until we're fully seated inside her. I feel her nails rake across my shoulders.

Keeping our thrusts slow is fucking torture. The friction of Matt's dick against mine as her pussy gets wetter and wetter, soaking us both, is enough to send me straight to the edge of no return. But I want, no need, to enjoy them both for more than thirty seconds.

"Oh, baby," I rumble against her lips.

Matt takes his turn. His kiss is dominating. We start thrusting faster into her as we take turns kissing her. All she can do is moan and pant. Her pussy pulses erratically as her wetness coats our cocks.

"Holy shit, beautiful," Matt moans. He looks down. "You're dripping for us. Do we feel that good?"

"Yes… Oh fuck, yes…" She clenches around us as we slide against each other, slamming into her. The sound of how wet she is rings in my ears and makes me even harder, but feeling Matt thicken inside her is what does me in.

I feel that familiar jolt shoot down my spine. My stomach tightens. Mariah trembles and shivers as she moans, pants, and writhes. Her pussy quivers and pulses for us.

Matt and I both press our lips against her neck as we pound deep and hard into her pussy over and over again.

"Ah!" she shouts, hanging onto us tighter. "Matt! DJ!"

"Come for us," we both rumble in unison against her neck.

"Ah! Matt! DJ!" she screams as her orgasm hits. She comes hard around us, soaking our dicks even more.

"Fuck!" I roar as I slam into her one last time. I come hard and deep in her pussy.

"My fuuuccckkk, baby girl," Matt rumbles. He slams into her one last time and comes hard and deep at the same time as I do. As she releases, she squeezes every last drop of come from our cocks.

"Oh God," she whispers. "Oh God."

We all pant against each other. Our dicks slide out of her. Matt glances at the couch and carries her over to it. We both plop down and snuggle our wife into us. As she usually does, she melts into us completely.

If anyone told my seventeen-year-old self that I would be in my fifties and married to the man and woman of my dreams, I would have them committed. When I met Matt, I thought I was the luckiest man on Earth.

When Mariah crashed her way into our lives, that something we'd been missing finally completed us. Now that I have Mariah and Matt, I feel like the puzzle of us is finished. My heart and soul soar with the love and contentment I feel emitting off of them.

And I know it radiates off of me for them.

This right here is everything I've ever needed.

Everything I've ever wanted and so much more.

This is my eternity.

Our always and forever.

The End

The Beautiful Dream Series

Available Now

Loving You
My Love, My Heart
Softening Lyric
Undercover Temptations
Captain Charming
Breaking Boundaries
Crashing Into You
Tactical Inferno
Ravishing Our Queen
Cherished By The Texan
Unveiling Our Passions

Box Sets Available

The Beautiful Dream Series: Box Set: Part 1
The Beautiful Dream Series: Box Set: Part 2

Other Books By Melony Ann
The Crane Family Series

Available Now

The Reluctant Mafia King
Sweet Lies
Billion Dollar Love Story
Be Mine
Protecting Her
Dangerously Forbidden Love
His Heart
Love In The Dark

Box Sets Available

The Crane Family Series

The Deimos Trilogy

Available Now

Connor's Legacy
Aryan's Alpha
Kade's Redemption

Box Sets Available

The Deimos Trilogy

The Forbidden Temptation Series

Available Now

The Detective's Forbidden Temptation
The Running Back's Forbidden Temptation

The Lucinio Family Series

Available Now

Rising From The Ashes
The Player's Rebel
Encrypting My Heart
Fighting My Fate

Multi Author Series
Piper Falls: Firehouse 49

Available Now

Ignite My Fire by Melony Ann
Regain My Fire by Kindra White
Playing With My Fire by D.L. Howe
Fight My Fire by Darley Collins
Against My Fire by Anneke Boshoff
Relight My Fire by Louise Murchie
Harness My Fire by Ayana Lisbet
Quench My Fire by Havana Wilder

Let's Be Friends

Follow me on

Bookbub

Facebook

Goodreads

Instagram

Tik Tok

Visit my website
www.melonyannauthor.com

Subscribe to my newsletter and get a FREE never-seen-before NOVELLA just for subscribers!
https://www.melonyannauthor.com/exclusive-content

Join my Facebook Reader Group!
Melony Ann's Sizzling Book Nook

The official Beautiful Dream Series Playlist on YouTube
https://youtube.com/playlist?list=PLGEiD5wbQmDe1z4_FeeKbMLcBkOz1M4L4

Dedication

In the darkest and scariest of times, you're our love and light.

Acknowledgements

Brad - My love for you grows more and more each day. Near or far, I know you're always with me. I'll love you forever.

Laura - I've always said you're the sunshine in my world. You kept me going through this book, proving my point that you really are my sunshine. I love you so, so much.

Jay - When I first met you, you were coming home from a deployment and dressed in your military uniform. Just as you guided me through the airport then, you continue to lead me now. I'll love you always.

Anneke - I can always count on you for an ear or a hug. You're always so amazing.

Jason - This book was the most difficult book I've ever written in my entire life. I wouldn't have gotten through it without you.

Kayla - You inspired me to go forward and write this. So, thank you. Thank you for being in my corner and helping me get this on paper.

To the Bookstagram Community.

To my family.

To all of those who believe in me and support me.

To all of those who don't.

Cover by: Carter Cover Designs

Edited by: Alyssa Skaggs

About Melony Ann

Melony Ann began writing short stories and poetry as a child. She continued honing her craft over the years until she took the plunge and began publishing her work, despite having severe anxiety.

Melony writes contemporary romance stories that are full of suspense and a lot of steam.

When she isn't writing, she is loving her family and working to make her life something she deserves.

Melony believes that if her writing can inspire just one person, then all of her hard work is worth it.

Her hope is that her writing allows each and every one of her readers to escape for a little while. To dive into a different world one book at a time.